CW00549611

How to Marry Harry

Nikki Perry & Kirsty Roby

1st edition, 2021

Edited by Evan Chan

Copyright © 2021 in text: Nikki Perry and Kirsty Roby

Nikki Perry and Kirsty Roby assert the moral right
to be identified as the authors of this work.

This is a work of fiction. Names, characters, businesses, places,
events and incidents are either the products of the author's imagination or used in a fictitious manner. Any resemblance to actual
persons, living or dead, or actual events is purely coincidental.

All rights reserved. Except for short extracts for the purpose of
review, no part of this book may be reproduced, stored in a re-
trieval system or transmitted in any form or by any means,
whether electronic, mechanical, photocopying, recording or otherwise, without prior written permission from the publisher.

ISBN 978-0-473-59462-6 (paperback)

ISBN 978-0-473-59464-0 (Kindle)

ISBN 978-0-473-59463-3 (Epub)

Cover design and layout by Yummy Book Covers

Typeset in Droid Serif, 10.5pt

To Anne,
for giving us Harry.

"When it comes to choosing between your
head and your heart, always choose your heart.
Your head knows everything and everyone,
but your heart only knows you."
— *Harry Styles*

Acknowledgements

Firstly, thank you, the reader, for taking a chance on us and reading this book. We hope you enjoy reading it as much as we enjoyed writing it.

Huge thanks to Dara Flaws, daughter, niece and fellow writer, who offered us amazingly helpful advice and didn't mock our first attempt at a novel. Without you we'd still be bumbling around in the dark.

Also, thanks to Kate and Martina as our first readers and cheerleaders, for all your encouragement and enthusiasm for our work.

Gratitude also to Karen McKenzie of Lighthouse PR for her wonderful help and expertise to get this book off our laptops and turned into a real book.

Thanks to Eva Chan for her quick and efficient editing and massive thanks to Enni of Yummy Book Covers for her gorgeous work.

For forgiving us for all the hours they were ignored while we talked for hours on the phone, big thanks and love to our families.

But our biggest thanks have to go to the gorgeous Mr Harry Styles who, without even realising it, set us down this path of writing.

How to Marry Harry

Prologue

As the coffin was carried up the elegant church aisle, Jo could feel Bobbi shaking beside her. Not, as you might expect, with grief, but with barely contained laughter. Jo couldn't look at her sister.

"Stop it," she hissed under her breath as she nudged her side. Bobbi let out a snort, tried to cover it as a sob. Their mother looked down the pew at them in bewilderment. She wasn't wearing her glasses so she hadn't noticed Donald, Uncle Bill's best friend and one of his pallbearers. He'd known Bill for years, and they'd both belonged to the New Zealand Scotsmen Society.

Donald had come in a kilt. And like a good Scot, he'd followed the rules about what went under it. He'd also managed to tuck the back of it into its tartan waist.

Donald was not a young man. Years of gravity meant Bobbi and Jo currently had a front-row view of Donald's wrinkly old testicles.

It was not a pretty sight.

◇

Jo looked across at her daughter Bayley, gorgeous in her black pantsuit. She smiled back and as she reached out to hold her mother's hand, her gaze caught Donald's visible family jewels, swaying from side to side, as he stepped up to place the coffin on the altar. Her face went white, then bright red. She looked at her mother in horror. Her mortified expression set Jo off. She couldn't help it. She dissolved into a fit of laughter that caused Bobbi and then Bayley to start giggling to themselves, like a line of well-dressed hyenas.

Their mother looked up from where she was making notes in her little purse pad. She was no doubt rating the flowers and the coffin's suitability for her own or their father's final show. Doreen loved a good funeral.

Thankfully, their father noticed Donald's exhibitionism, doing a quick tug on his kilt to cover the pendulous scrotum, and they managed to pull themselves together for the rest of the service.

◇

It was actually a lovely ceremony and the music Bill had chosen was an eclectic mix of bagpipes, hymns and something modern Bobbi and Jo hadn't recognised. Bayley informed them it was Harry Styles — 'Sign of the Times'.

They'd done the tea and club sandwiches and now they were at Jo's having a drink.

"Here's to Uncle Bill," said Bobbi.

"And may we never see another baggy ball-bag like that again," added Jo.

"Well, now we know what's under the kilts."

They both shuddered theatrically.

It was almost enough to put you off Scotsmen for life.

CHAPTER 1

Jo

Group message to: Bobbi, Bayley
Jo: Have you seen how hot harry styles is now?
8.29pm

Bobbi : Who?
8.31pm

Bayley: FFS, mother!
Don't you think he's a bit young for you? You're spending too much time alone.
9.59pm

Bobbi: Oh, I just googled. Cute!
10.03pm

Jo sipped her third coffee of the day and idly scanned through her emails. There were two new ones since she'd last looked, one from a clothing company trying to convince her to buy a pair of patterned lounge pants, so her life would be complete, and the other from Uncle Bill's lawyer. She deleted the first one and contemplated the second.

Uncle Bill had been married to their mother's late sister Avis and had left Jo and Bobbi a small legacy — and a task to complete. He wanted his ashes to be returned to the town in Scotland he had grown up in and he'd left them some money for a trip to do this. Instead of reading it, Jo opened a new window and typed in 'Harry Styles, Falling, music video'.

Message to Bobbi
Jo: https://www.youtube.com/watch?v=1Y
Harry Styles Performs a Crosswalk Concert
10.01pm

https://www.youtube.com/watch?v=VF-r5TtiT9w
Harry Styles — Adore You (Official Video)
10.23pm

https://www.youtube.com/watch?v=jIIuzB11dsA
Harry Styles: NPR Music Tiny Desk Concert
Such a lovely voice. I could listen to him talk all night.
11.59pm

Bobbi: It sounds like you did. What time did you go to bed? That drummer rocks it though. She's so good

9.42am

Cute jumper BTW

9.44am

The house was quiet. It had been quiet before Marcus had left, and now it was just her. She'd found out he'd been cheating on her and that it wasn't the first time. Now he'd moved in with his current girlfriend and her two young children and the thought of how that must be going made Jo almost cheerful; Marcus had never been particularly tolerant of small children.

Sure, she was sad that her marriage was over, he was the father of her child after all, but she had been surprised to realise how relieved she was as well. Jo had to admit they hadn't been happy for years and Marcus had worn down her self-esteem. She used to be a fun person but she'd become more quiet and withdrawn around him. It had just been easier than dealing with his moods.

She put Harry's latest album on and turned it up nice and loud.

In the midst of unloading the dishwasher and wondering whether she could be bothered having a shower, the phone rang. Glancing at the incoming number she could see it was Bobbi so she picked up. They usually spoke at least a couple of times a week.

"Jo, have you spoken to Mum today?" Bobbi very rarely bothered with any preamble or introduction.

"No, I'm trying not to. Why?"

There was a dramatic sigh at the other end. "Oh, the usual. Dad had what was probably indigestion but could be a heart attack and should she make an urgent appointment with the doctor? He insisted it was because she put too much cream in the seafood chowder. Then she was wondering which funeral home she'd use if he ended up succumbing, and it wouldn't be the one Shirley Campbell used for her husband because they got his sister's name wrong. I can't figure out whether she's genuinely worried for Dad's health or just looking forward to throwing a party."

Shutting the dishwasher door, Jo tucked the phone under her chin and started to wipe down the kitchen bench before taking the phone and her cup of tea into the living room where she sunk onto the sofa, her feet tucked under her.

"The latter, I would say."

"Anyway, are you okay? You seem to be coming a bit unhinged. First you're sending me cat videos, then photos of chocolate-dipped pickles — what were they like, by the way?"

"Not quite how I imagined, but not terrible either. I'd never thought of making them till now. Marcus hated pickles."

"Another black mark against him," Bobbi muttered. "So, what's with the obsession with this Harry Styles?"

"I wouldn't call it an obsession," Jo said indignantly. "I've just had a bit of time on my hands and I'm really loving his music. And he seems so nice and quite adorable really."

"So you like his music but you just happen to like to look at the videos while you're listening?" Bobbi chuckled.

"No. Well, not just that. I've also downloaded both his albums and I listen to them when I'm walking. His voice is mesmerising."

"Well, I'm not judging. I started looking for recipes using eggplant the other night and ended up two hours later Google-stalking Curtis Stigers' house. He lives in Boise, Idaho, just FYI."

"Did you know eggplants are actually a berry?" Jo informed her.

"Or an emoji," Bobbi said drily.

◇

By the time she hung up it was well into mid-morning. The day stretched ahead, but not unpleasantly. Jo had always been a bit of a homebody and worked from home as a proofreader.

She hadn't really admitted to herself that ever since Bayley had left home to study to be a chef, she was still trying to find a purpose for herself. She'd spent all those years being someone's mum, someone's wife, a daughter, a friend to people she both knew well and didn't really know at all. Who was she? Who had she even been before? What music did she used to love? What books did she read that weren't for work?

She and Marcus had been together since she was twenty-one and they'd gotten married and had Bayley within two years. Being young and impressionable, she'd formed her opinions around his, but over the past few years had found she didn't always agree with him. Actually that was probably an understatement. Then he'd played his hand. She was just now beginning to realise hers wasn't the losing one. Now, there was a trip to the United Kingdom to look forward to and plan.

Flipping open her laptop she googled 'Top things to do in the UK'.

Her only trip to Europe had been just before she'd met Marcus when she'd gone on her OE with a friend from school. They'd done a budget tour which involved what felt like 200 countries in four days, drinking anything cheap, shagging as many of the single guys on the tour as they could (kudos if you bagged the tour guide) and then sleeping on the bus and missing most of the sights along the way because they were so hungover.

The follow-up to this was living in a dingy flat in London with two other Kiwis and an Aussie girl, which was so outrageously expensive that she and Lisa had shared a room to reduce the rent. Jo had been working as a nanny six days a week and she'd been so miserable she'd come home after six months.

But this time it would be different. This time she was

interested in culture and history, scenery and eating good food. And she'd be travelling with Bobbi, who was interested in the same things, unlike Marcus, whose idea of a fabulous holiday was to go to Fiji and relax at the resort pool for a week, eat expensive, uninspired food, and drink wine that had good reviews. Then he'd book an all-day fishing trip, seemingly forgetting that she got horribly seasick but still insisting that it was something they should do together.

She copied a few links for ideas for the trip and sent them to Bobbi, along with a 'Harry Styles smiling' compilation and a particularly nice photo of him she'd come across on Instagram.

After lunch she put in a few hours of work and went for a walk before having dinner and a glass of wine.

Then Jo pulled out her wedding album and flicked it open to a random page. Several of the photos already had doodles drawn on them. Marcus had a purple mullet in one and now she drew a moustache on her ex-mother-in-law and hummed happily to herself. It was kind of like scrapbooking, she reasoned, blacking out one of her ex-husband's teeth.

She topped up her glass and was sitting contentedly on her sofa, checking her Facebook messages. There was one from Bayley.

Mother, please stop sending me Harry links. I do not need to know that we have the same favourite book. YOU also don't need to know all these personal things about him.

Bayley: Are you OK?

9.52pm

Jo: Do you not like him? And I'm absolutely fine, thanks for asking

10.37pm

Bayley: He seems perfectly charming and very talented. I like his solo music

10.45pm

Jo: That accent, I could listen to him talking for the rest of my life. He'd make a lovely boyfriend for you

10.45pm

Bayley: Well ... if you can organise that I wouldn't say no haha-hahahahaha :)

10.50pm

Jo: I'll work on it. Can be my new hobby. How is everything with you? Are you getting enough sleep and taking your iron tablets?

10.51pm

Wriggling her shoulders, Jo opened another Google window and while checking the time caught a glimpse of herself in the mirror hung above the sideboard. Her hair looked slightly dishevelled, fringe a little too long, and the cardigan she'd thrown on had a large hole in one arm. It was almost midnight and she had been online for hours. She reached for the bottle of wine and was surprised to find it empty. But there was a bottle of Frangelico unopened in the cupboard and that would make a good little nightcap.

Too easy to drink though, she realised, as she poured the second one and typed 'harry styles, live performance schedule' into the Google search.

March. That would be a lovely time to visit the United Kingdom. And if the dates didn't work out, well, it's not like the tickets would be unsellable. Before she could change her mind, Jo clicked a few times and then pulled out her credit card to check the security number.

◇

The next morning Jo sat in her home office gazing out the window. She was about a quarter of the way through proofreading a very tedious book titled 'Manuals, Guidelines and Standards for Meat Processing in New Zealand'. It paid the bills, and she could pretty much work the hours she wanted but she felt it would be a lot more interesting if she were proofreading bodice-rippers or even autobiographies of famous people, rather than learning how important it was to have the right grinder for processing dog food. She did have to concede that because of her work, she now had a better than average knowledge of things that most people had no interest in knowing anything about.

There was a ding in her Inbox and pleased for an excuse for a break, she clicked 'View'.

Thank you very much for purchasing tickets for Harry Styles Love On Tour

She went upstairs to make a coffee and decided to ring Bobbi.

"Hi, it's me," she said when Bobbi answered.

"I know it's you, I can see you on my caller ID. You're getting as bad—"

"— as Mum. I know."

"So, what's up? You're not working?"

"I am. I can only handle about an hour before I start to feel like I'm going to have nightmares about falling into a boiler and nobody realising until scraps of my clothing are found in someone's dog roll. How are things at the bar?"

Bobbi had been running 'Bob's Your Aunt' as a cabaret bar for five years, since her partner Leo left it to her. They had gotten together when Leo was in his early sixties and Bobbi in her thirties and nobody was more surprised than the two of them when Bobbi had become pregnant. But she had lost the baby fairly late into the pregnancy and their focus after that had been the bar. She hadn't let it show to many people but she was devastated when Leo had died.

Now Bobbi ran the bar with the help of Sam, her fantastic manager. Bayley had just started working there as a sous chef, which was great, but Jo sometimes felt a little jealous that her sister saw more of her daughter than she did.

"Everything's pretty good. I've just signed up a fabulous Stevie Nicks tribute act. You'll have to come down and stay soon."

"I'd like to see that. We can do some planning for the trip too," Jo said quickly, and then added, "Speaking of, you'll never believe who is doing a UK tour next year."

There was a very brief silence.

"I think I can probably hazard a guess," Bobbi answered drily.

"It's Harry Styles," Jo enthused, unnecessarily. "So, will you come with me? Just one little concert. Please say you will."

"Well, if the alternative is sitting in a hotel bar drinking by myself ..."

"Great. It'll be fun."

"I guess I can hope that he might wear one of those open shirts. I do like the tattoos, I must say."

Jo leant her elbows on the table and cupped her free hand around her coffee mug.

"So, you've been looking at the links I've sent you then." She tried not to sound too smug. "I have to say, I'm not a fan of tattoos. I really don't like that giant moth on his torso."

Bobbi sputtered a laugh. Jo loved the sound of her sister's laugh and even though she knew Bobbi couldn't see her, she smiled back in return.

"It's a butterfly," Bobbi said. "Obviously."

"It looks like a moth to me," Jo shuddered. She'd always hated moths. Bobbi knew it and as a child she would torture Jo with them by chasing her around the house with one of the gigantic, hideous things cupped in her hand. If she got close enough to Jo, she'd then release it practically in her face.

"Perhaps you could lay your hands on Harry's butterfly tattoo. It might be good therapy to cure your fear."

"*Bobbi!* You do realise how young he is? I was thinking more son-in-law material than boyfriend."

They both pondered this for a few seconds and then at exactly the same time exclaimed: "But it's a fine line."

CHAPTER 2

Bobbi

"Which one of you hoes left their fuck-me boots in the hall-way?" Bobbi shouted as she manoeuvred around the offend-ing footwear on her way to the storeroom with the last of the gin delivery.

Owning a bar with a drag night cabaret was fun, but some-times it felt like the queens were just too much chaos, even for her. It wasn't the boots or wigs so much as the bitchy ar-guments and high drama over who was better at their make-up, or who had stolen whose boobs. Sometimes she felt like she was the most masculine chick in the building. And that was saying something, considering her rack.

When Leo had died, she felt quite daunted by the pros-pect of taking over the business. There was so much more paperwork than she'd realised. She was used to running the bar, managing the queens and being a social face to the customers, not doing wages, taxes and insurance. Leo had left things in a little bit of a mess and it had taken her a few years to sort out, but finally it was running smoothly and she'd ironed out a lot of the kinks.

In some ways, the learning curve had been a welcome distraction from losing Leo. His death had rattled her. She'd had to get used to being on her own again.

They had slowly grown into their relationship. Bobbi had always teased Leo that he'd just worn her down. He'd had a thing for her when she first started working for him in her twenties, behind the bar. They'd never married, but when they did move in together, that was when Leo had renamed the bar for her. His big romantic gesture. She'd done a lot of wild, spontaneous stuff before they became a couple. She had a lot of fun, experimented a bit with guys and partying, but Leo had always been there, kind, steady, and adoring. It hadn't been mad passion, more like a comfortable pair of boots than sexy heels. But they'd genuinely liked each other, enjoyed each other's company, talked about books, liked cooking together, even liked the same music surprisingly, although Bobbi's musical taste did tend to lean towards the old classics rather than modern.

Although now, she found herself humming along to 'Meet Me in the Hallway' every time she came down here thanks to Jo and her constant music links. That damn Harry was wearing her down.

Still, he was a bloody nice-looking kid, with some serious talent, so if Bayley was keen, she might actually be a perfect fit for him. Her niece was gorgeous, talented, funny and smart and probably Bobbi's favourite person ever. Even if she was biased. But she was as close as Bobbi had to her own kid, and if she wanted Harry, Bobbi would try to give him to her.

She'd never really planned to have kids. She loved them. Had even thought about teaching at one stage, but she'd never planned for her own. If she really thought about it, maybe it was just that she always thought she had more time. Even now in her forties, she felt like she was in her late twenties. It was only when she got out of bed wrong and something twinged, or she had to rummage in her handbag for her reading glasses, that she felt her age.

Before Leo, none of her relationships had lasted long enough to consider having a kid with them. That possibly reflected on her taste in men at the time, she supposed. She'd always gone for the bad boys, and they didn't make for family men much.

When Bay was born, she was smitten. She adored that kid from the moment she arrived in the world. She changed nappies and fed her solids, took hundreds of photos and showed them to everyone she knew. She went to every birthday party with the 'fun aunty' gift in tow. She went to as many of her school things as she could, babysat whenever Jo would let her. Rode roller-coasters and played tea parties and watched *Ice Age* over and over. Bayley was the love of her life.

It was a shame Jo hadn't had more kids. She was an amazing mum, and she would have suited having half a dozen babies. But she'd had trouble conceiving after Bay, and then Bobbi suspected things had gone a little south in the marriage. She wouldn't have put it past Marcus to have gone off and got a sneaky snip even. He was never much into the fatherhood thing. But he always made out like there was likely something wrong with Jo. Bobbi had never really warmed to Marcus. She'd tried to get along with him, but he didn't make it easy.

Bobbi had had a few occasions to worry as a young woman about unplanned pregnancies, but never got pregnant, so she'd sort of assumed she might not be fertile. When she found out she was expecting, she was as shocked as anyone. Nicely shocked though. And excited. Leo perhaps hadn't been quite so enthusiastic — he had grown-up kids from his first marriage — so he wasn't looking forward to going back to nappies and sleepless nights, but he was supportive and happy for Bobbi.

When they lost the baby, it was the worst pain Bobbi had ever known.

They'd even tried again after a few months, but without success. She tried not to dwell too much, but it lingered still, like a dull ache.

She was lucky Jo had shared Bayley with her. Bloody lucky to have Jo in general really; they were best friends as well as sisters.

They'd done some random, slightly crazy stuff in the past, so the idea that someone as famous and adored as Harry Styles might pick her niece from the billions of wannabes in the world might be far-fetched, but Bobbi was a romantic at heart. There was someone for everyone, right? So who was to say that a small town girl from New Zealand wouldn't be Harry's Ms Right? All they had to do was help lead him to her.

She was mulling over a few more ideas for that when Polly-Esther yelled out to tell her there was a large parcel for her to sign. Plan A had arrived.

Last summer Bobbi had snapped a fantastic photo of Bayley in her skimpy red bikini and had the picture enlarged onto a full-sized cardboard cutout. All it would take was for Harry to spot her niece during the concert and he would be smitten. And surely he'd have to notice this.

It was a little more ungainly than she had anticipated though. As she carried it up to her apartment, she did wonder how she would get it on the plane, or into cabs and things. Still, it would be worth it.

Downstairs, she found Sam in the small industrial kitchen talking quietly to Bayley as she prepped for the dinner service.

Sam had been managing the place for almost six years now, and she was bloody lucky to have him. The customers loved him, and the queens all tried desperately to hook up with him. She'd never heard any gossip about his love life since he'd started behind the bar at twenty-two, and he took his job very seriously. The place would be in great hands while she was away with Jo, and she was starting to look forward to it more and more as they planned. She and Jo had done several holidays together and they always had a blast. Although, thinking about the last time they'd done a trip away and Jo had made them stay in an old converted women's prison, she made a mental note to ask what accommodation they had booked so far.

Her phone dinged with a message and she opened it to see another Harry pic.

Rolling her eyes, she showed Bayley her phone. "Another shot of your Mr Right, Bayleaf, courtesy of your Harry-obsessed mother."

She watched Bayley's face as she took in the photo and laughed at the blush that crept over her.

"Help me, Sam," she cried.

Sam just smirked and said, "Well, he is pretty gorgeous, Bay, and so are you."

Bayley turned even pinker, and Bobbi thought, Harry really would love her.

"Your mum and I will get him to fall in love with you, Bay, but when you and Harry hook up, I want to be thanked in the wedding speech, okay?"

Bayley seemed to be concentrating very hard on cutting up her peppers.

"Right now, Auntie Bob, I'm more worried about finding somewhere to live than someone to marry."

"What? Why? What's wrong with your flat?

"The landlord is selling and wants to do it up first so we have to be out next month."

"Well, why don't you move in here till you find somewhere? I've got two rooms."

"Yeah but you'll be away for a month soon, and isn't Sam staying at yours?" Bayley looked up and across at Sam as she spoke.

"Well sure, but he won't mind, will you, Sam? You're both always here working anyway, it'd make life easy."

Sam raised his eyebrows and then studied his nails.

"Ah, yeah, nah, that's cool. I mean, it's your apartment. I'm just glad to stay rent free for a month. It's still free, right?"

"Yes, Sam, free. So long as you don't burn the place down or run it into the ground. I know you're saving for a house deposit, so it's all good. Your mum will probably appreciate the break too."

Bayley shrugged. "Well, yeah, maybe then, if I can't find anything else. Is it free for mc too, my favourite aunty ever?"

Bobbi laughed. "Only if you deep-fry some pickles tonight and then come up to watch *The Princess Bride* with me after your shift."

"Deal," Bayley said, "now get out of my kitchen."

"As you wish," Bobbi grinned.

◇

As she headed back into the bar, a pink wig poked its head out of the second door and asked, "Boss, any chance you've got a spare pair of falsies lying around?" and Bobbi couldn't help but think a holiday was just what she needed. Thanks, Uncle Bill. And perhaps she'd meet a hot Scotsman to entertain her for a while.

◇

Her phone dinged again and Bobbi roared with laughter when she opened the link Jo had sent her: an image of Harry in a kilt. Sometimes their sister telepathy was scary.

CHAPTER 3

Bayley

"You hate the idea, don't you?" Bayley scrutinised Sam's face as she asked. "I can find somewhere else if you do. I'll stay with a friend or something." Sam still hadn't said a word, and it was making her nervous.

Finally he sighed. "I don't hate it, Bay. Quite the opposite."

Was he blushing? It was hard to tell with his olive skin, but he looked like he was going to say something else, so she waited.

The silence stretched out between them.

What had he meant anyway? That he liked the idea of them being roommates? That he liked her? That was probably wishful thinking though. Bayley had had a crush on him for years, since he'd started at Bob's Your Aunt when she was sixteen. He always treated her like an annoying little cousin. Well, until she'd started in the kitchen, and then they started to become more like friends. It was just that now he seemed to have friend-zoned her and Bayley was determined to move them to a different level.

Sam was her ideal man. He had a dry sense of humour, the king of the well-placed one-liner. He was goal oriented like her and encouraging of her dreams, and, as a bonus, he was nice looking. He wasn't that tall, which suited Bayley, considering she was on the short side. He had great arms, from lifting kegs and from rock climbing on his days off, and dreamy chocolate-brown eyes with dark lashes.

He'd also been a great sounding board for her during her parents' split. Plus, he gave a great hug. Finally he spoke. "Move in, Bay. It'll be fine. Really."

He didn't look at her though, and then he said; "I'd better get on with stuff," and Bayley felt like she'd fucked up. That she should have said something else. She opened her mouth to call out to him and realised she had no idea what else to say.

Maybe, though, this was her opportunity. If she was living in the same apartment as him she might be able to make him see that she'd grown up, was a woman, that she wanted him. She was going to have to assert herself, she decided. She was good at that, after all. When she set her mind to something, she usually got it.

She was going to do it. Make her move. Shit. She needed to go shopping for new, sexier underwear. When she got paid.

As a bonus, aside from the plus of seeing Sam every morning and night, the free rent would help her knock some debt off her credit card. She still had her student loan to pay off and her mum had lent her money for her kitchen knives too.

She missed her mum. She was looking forward to seeing her before they flew out to the UK. She'd said she was planning to come down a few nights earlier and they'd get a few days to hang out. They were getting to a cool phase now where they'd become more like friends than mum and daughter in some ways. They could go out for cocktails, or shopping, have lunch and talk about stuff that might have been weird a few years ago. Still, she was always there for Bayley in mum mode. They were close, she and her mum. More so than her dad. It was weird now, talking to Marcus, with Jayden and Ella running around in the background. He told her he'd like her to think of the kids as her siblings, but they weren't. They were only young, and Bayley wasn't that keen on little kids. She felt a bit jealous when Marcus talked about them and parented them. He'd never been that invested in her childhood, had been absent a lot, so it was a bit galling to Bayley hearing about him doing school pick-ups and activities with them. He'd never talked to Bayley about the cheating either, and it pissed her off that he didn't seem to think he'd done anything wrong.

But their split had had the opposite effect with Bayley and her mum. They'd gotten closer. Talked more often, and more honestly.

She thought her mum was a bit nuts over this crazy thing

with her and Harry Styles, but, she figured she'd leave her to it. It was something for her to focus on, and she needed something since the split. Plus, she and Aunty Bob would be travelling and having fun, and they were going for Uncle Bill, not just to see Harry Styles, so it seemed harmless enough. She did like Harry's music, and he was gorgeous obviously. She wouldn't mind seeing him in concert, but she wasn't going to tell her mum that and encourage her. She kind of wished she was going with them in some ways. They had said she could, but they had been talking about a Vietnam trip before Uncle Bill had died and she'd far rather join them for that. All that food!

Bayley loved food. Even as a toddler her mum said she would eat stuff other kids screwed their noses up at. Avocado, prawns, chilli, curry, blue cheese. She'd known right from high school that she wanted to be a chef. Food science had been her best subject at school and it was a given she'd apply to do a chef's course when she left. One day, she'd run her own kitchen. Or maybe a food truck.

For now, she was happy learning, so she got back to her prepping, and her plans to finally get her man.

CHAPTER 4

Bobbi

Bobbi was an organiser. She knew it was far too early to pack, but she still couldn't help herself from putting her bag and a few bits and pieces on the bed in her spare room. She'd end up packing and repacking at least three times.

When she'd gone on an African safari with a friend she had been packed ready to go a month before. But it made a trip seem more real to slowly add toiletries and new undies and things to her growing pile.

Bobbi wore a lot of bright colours, and now she couldn't decide if she should pack something black for when they got to Scotland and had the ash-scattering 'thing'. What was it even called? she mused. A ceremony? Service? Memorial? And did it matter if she wasn't in black? It would only be her and Jo, she imagined. Still, she messaged her sister anyway to check her thoughts on it.

Jo sent back a quick reply to say she'd thought she'd just use her black travel pants and asked Bobbi what coat she was taking. She also sent another video of Harry doing carpool karaoke with James Corden. She'd watch that later.

Now, she threw in a little black dress she had that wasn't too sparkly. It also wasn't that little, she thought wryly, because Bobbi wasn't either, but it was batwinged and quite flattering. She could use that as a double-up if they went anywhere fancy, she reasoned.

◇

She and Jo had been close to Uncle Bill. He and Avis had lived about half an hour away, and never had kids. They'd never really been told why that was. Avis had been quite a modern woman for her time and worked as a bookkeeper, even after they married. She had died in her fifties and Bill had been on his own after that. He'd been a history teacher at the local high school, known to be strict and a bit grumpy, but as kids, Jo and Bobbi had always loved seeing him because of the magic trick he did where a coin appeared from behind their ear. He'd always do it twice so that there was a coin for each of them.

As soon as they could get away, they'd jump on their Raleigh 20 bikes and take off for the local dairy to get a fifty-cent bag of lollies each. Then they'd sit on the bus stop bench and eat them all before they went home, where Uncle Bill would always say 'And where did your coins go, lassies?'

and they would feign innocence, claiming they'd lost them. Bill would always reply, "It must be magic then," and laugh his big laugh.

Even after decades in New Zealand, he'd still had a thick Scottish accent that they'd both loved. As adults, they had enjoyed Bill's company whenever they saw him. He'd been very book smart, and full of interesting trivia for Jo. Bobbi had loved the wealth of good stories he had about naughty students he'd taught. He'd even come to the bar to check out the show once or twice. And he loved a drink.

There was a shriek and a smashing of glass downstairs. Bobbi left her packing and reminiscing and headed down to the bar to see what the drama (queen) was. Sometimes she envied Jo her quiet, peaceful life.

◊

They picked up Uncle Bill's ashes the day before they flew out. The crematorium office was only a twenty-minute drive from the city so they took Bobbi's little Mini for a spin.

When they arrived, Jo, who had white-knuckled the passenger handle the entire way, let out a dramatic sigh. Bobbi ignored her. Her driving may have been slightly erratic, but it had hardly been a death-defying experience in her opinion.

The receptionist was a Goth-looking young lady with jet-black hair, piercings in her eyebrow, ears and lip, and a death metal T-shirt. She was chewing a wad of gum and her rather informal greeting of "'Sup?" wasn't quite what they'd been expecting. Her name tag read 'LAKE'.

After explaining who they were collecting, Lake disappeared out the back to retrieve Uncle Bill while they waited.

"Did you know, in Mongolia, the lama leads the burial procession and they're the only one who can touch the dead body?" Jo informed her.

"How would a llama know where to go?"

"Lama, Bobbi, not a llama," snorted Jo, "as in spiritual leader, not crazy-haired animal."

They were still discussing pronunciation of the two words when Lake returned, carrying a small brown cardboard box.

She handed it over and Bobbi couldn't help feeling like she was getting a doggy bag from a diner. 'Uncle Bill's leftovers,' she thought, trying not to laugh.

They signed off some paperwork and took some forms before getting back into the Mini and whipping home to the bar. They found Bayley in the kitchen making stock. She leaned over Bobbi's shoulder, looked at the ashes, and frowned.

"What's wrong?" Bobbi asked.

"Did you bother to read the label on the box before you left?" Bayley asked.

Bobbi and Jo looked at each other.

Bayley snorted. "This is classic, you guys, you've been given the wrong person."

"What do you mean the *wrong* person?" Bobbi looked puzzled.

"Well, unless Uncle Bill also goes by the name Albert Winters, I don't think that's him in the box."

Bobbi and Jo both peered over her shoulder to read the label.

"Fuck."

Lake had mixed up the ashes, they assumed. They'd have to go back and swap Albert for Bill.

Bayley was still giggling. "You should have checked."

"Well, you don't expect to be given the wrong person," Bobbi said defensively.

"It makes you wonder how many people who have been buried under rose bushes or scattered at sea aren't really who their loved ones thought they were," Jo mused.

They both sighed heavily and Bobbi picked up the ashes. She snared a chunk of carrot from the chopping board.

"Come on, Albert," Bobbi grumbled. "Bloody Lake. If she spent less time on her eyeliner and more time focusing on her job, this would never have happened. What a pain in the arse."

"Or you could have looked," Bayley reminded her unhelpfully. Bobbi shot Bayley a baleful glare.

"I hope someone else hasn't picked Bill up already," said Jo, sounding slightly alarmed.

"We'd better hurry then."

"I'm driving," Jo insisted.

CHAPTER 5

Jo

Things never seemed to go smoothly for Jo and Bobbi when they travelled together. Once, before Bobbi got her glasses, they'd accidentally boarded the wrong plane and been detained by security to ensure they weren't a terrorist threat. Another time they got on a tour bus to an Amish village instead of the regular coach to Philadelphia. Although, she had to say, it had been very educational. They'd ended up in a place called Intercourse, where the town's welcome sign had been a great photo opportunity and the souvenir shop was brilliant for getting gifts. Bobbi still had a bumper sticker on her Mini.

So when things went a little pear-shaped the day they left for the UK, it shouldn't really have been a surprise to anyone.

First, the Uber had been forced to make a dangerous U-turn when Bobbi realised she'd left cardboard Bayley behind. Then the airline staff were dubious about them taking her on board for the domestic flight.

"We wouldn't normally accept this ... er ... sort of item as hand luggage," the attendant said.

"We couldn't possibly check her in," Jo replied horrified. "You can't expect my daughter to travel in the cargo space."

"Right, well, there's no time to check her in now." The attendant looked like she wasn't going to budge and Jo worried they'd have to leave Bayley behind. She glanced at Bobbi, who had that look in her eye. The one she got when she'd had a brilliant idea. Sometimes these ideas weren't actually so brilliant. Luckily, this was not one of those times.

Bobbi sniffled dramatically and leant over to the attendant, Gill.

"Gill, sweetheart, my poor sister lost her daughter two months ago. I'm begging you, if you could find somewhere to put her effigy, you'll make a grieving mum very happy."

Jo wiped a fake tear from her eye for good measure and tried to look mournful.

Gill's face flushed slightly. "I'll see what I can do."

She took Bayley into the cockpit in the end. Jo hoped she wasn't going to be a distraction to the pilots in any way.

◇

Then there was the incident at the international airport. Jo took Uncle Bill's ashes out of her bag looking for her passport and left him beside her on one of the chairs.

She always felt slightly jittery before they flew. It was a mix of anticipation and the thought of the boredom of the long flight ahead. Which was why Bobbi suggested they head to the bar for a drink and a loaded bowl of wedges to 'settle their nerves' and of course to toast Bill.

Jo rummaged in her bag for her wallet for a quick second drink. "Shit."

"Shit what?"

"We've lost Uncle Bill."

"You've only just realised? He's been gone for months now, Josie. We wouldn't be here otherwise, would we?"

"No, you idiot. I've *lost* him. As in, the remaining bits of him. I think I left him downstairs, at those seats."

"Oh, for fuck's sake. You'd better go and get him then."

"Can you come too?" Jo pleaded. Bobbi sighed and gave her a long-suffering look before downing the rest of her drink and gathering up her belongings.

Uncle Bill was not where they had left him.

"Shit," Jo said again. She turned to a couple who were sitting a few seats away. "I left my uncle sitting here, in a box, about half an hour ago. You haven't seen him, have you?"

"Not our live uncle," Bobbi interjected in a helpful manner.

The couple looked at each other with something like stupefaction. They seemed to be having one of those wordless conversations that couples have with their eyes.

"No, sorry, I can't say we have."

Jo got down on her hands and knees to have a last sweep

under the row of seats, just to make sure he hadn't fallen underneath. "Uncle Bill," she called, "are you there?" The couple quickly gathered their belongings and moved off, muttering something about allowing plenty of time before their flight.

They trudged to security and were redirected to lost and found, which was unattended. Jo impatiently dinged the bell three separate times with no luck. They could see the little brown box sitting on a shelf against the back wall and were debating who would leap over the counter to retrieve it when a grumpy-looking woman finally appeared out of the back room, looking as though they'd interrupted her dinner break. She smelt like tuna.

Despite Jo and Bobbi explaining about the ashes, she still made them produce paperwork from the crematorium.

"Who would try to claim some random person's ashes?" Bobbi queried. The woman merely shrugged and disappeared back through the door.

As a result, they were a little later getting through customs than they'd intended and nearly missed the flight. It felt like everyone was giving them filthy looks as they made their way up the aisle.

"Someone has to be last on," Bobbi retorted loudly.

Bayley proved to be a bit problematic again too, the cut-out Bayley, that is, not the real one. Luckily, a kind flight attendant offered to store her for the duration of the trip. She was a Harry fan, bless her. They had the window and middle seat, squeezing past a rather beefy man in the aisle seat who smelt strongly of BO.

The small child in front of them kept looking through the gap in the seats, standing to peer over the top and giggling at them, making it very hard for Jo to concentrate on her book. Bobbi made a scary, deranged face. The child burst into noisy sobs for a good twenty minutes, but at least it stopped him from annoying them for the rest of the trip.

On the lay-over in Hong Kong, Jo ate some pork and cabbage dumplings, which caused her to have gas for the first few hours of the next leg. After a few too many glasses of wine, they laughed far too much until an attendant asked them to please settle down. Jo thought this was a little unreasonable of him, and said as much. After all, he'd been the one to give them the wine in the first place. Bobbi snored loudly and Jo hardly slept. The large man next to her kept giving her odd looks as she watched a movie and hummed to herself; that was the problem with airplane headphones, you couldn't really tell how loud you were. Her arse was sore from sitting for so long.

If only we could just portal to where we wanted to go, Jo thought. She'd have been willing to pay quadruple if that were possible.

◇

Jo heard Bobbi give a loud yawn beside her as she gazed out the window of the cab. Not a black London cab, to her disappointment, but just a regular taxi, the young dreadlocked driver playing, of all things, classical music.

"Fuck me, I can't wait to have a shower and lie down flat in a real bed. I smell like something's crawled up my fanny and died," Bobbi grumbled. "And it's bloody cold."

"I forget how much I hate those long flights. And how I should just drink water." Jo pressed her fingers into her temples. "Did you know the air on planes is literally as dry as the Sahara?"

"I did not," Bobbi answered.

"I think I have a hangover," Jo whined. "And I smell of sweat from our seatmate." She raised her left arm and sniffed her armpit, then did the same with her right, as though they might both smell different.

"I think that pong is all you, not big Alan, and he didn't seem to appreciate your falling asleep and drooling on him, to be honest."

"Liar. I didn't."

"You bloody did. But I think he was too scared to move in case you started drunk singing again."

"Poor Alan. I hope he didn't think I was hitting on him." Jo was mortified at the thought.

"Nah, he was gay, so he was safe from your charms," Bobbi said knowledgeably.

Jo laughed. "How do you know that?"

Bobbi looked affronted. "I've told you before, Jo, I have excellent gaydar."

Jo was dubious but said nothing and leaned back against the headrest.

◇

It seemed an eternity and the meter was ticking over at a furious rate, but finally the taxi pulled up at an unassuming-looking little hotel in Covent Garden. The brickwork was white with freshly painted black trim. A pot of bright-red gerberas hung from a jaunty sign announcing the hotel's name.

Bobbi paid the driver and he leapt out to assist them with their baggage. They'd packed minimally and only had a small suitcase each. As he lifted out the cardboard cutout of Bayley, he gave her a quick glance and grinned. "Here, don't forget your daughter."

Jo grabbed her suitcase and wrestled with her large handbag and jacket.

"I don't know why she has to be so scantily dressed," she grumbled, awkwardly hoisting Bayley under her arm.

Bobbi looked witheringly at her. "Bayley would look stunning in a jute sack, but obviously we need to go for maximum effect. She's going to have to stand out from the crowd." She patted her cutout niece fondly on the head. "She looks like she got a fucking lot more sleep than us. I reckon that lovely attendant put her in the crew sleeping area. Maybe she's even been travelling business class."

She pushed the door open and held it while Jo shuffled inside in a most inelegant manner.

◇

Bobbi flopped down on one of the single beds while Jo propped Bayley carefully against the wall and plugged in her phone to charge. The room was blandly decorated in shades of brown and cream, and 'cosy' to say the least. The bathroom was so small that you had to practically stand on the peach-coloured toilet seat to close the door.

"Right," said Jo, "we need to shower and get something to eat."

Bobbi groaned. "I just want to go to sleep. But yeah, we've got to try to acclimatise, I guess. Get our mindset into local time." She hauled herself up and started pulling things out of her bag. "What's the plan anyway? When's the concert and how many days do we have in London?"

Jo felt slightly uncomfortable. "Weeell, ..." She fiddled with the zip on her suitcase, acting as though it were stuck to avoid looking at her sister. "We've got tomorrow here, then we go to Birmingham for the show."

"Birmingham? Why the fuck did you pick Birmingham?"

"That was the first show. I just clicked and bought tickets. But, the industrial heritage sounds ... interesting ... and they have canals apparently. That could be fun."

Jo's phone chimed several times. "Shit, three missed calls from Mum."

Bobbi checked hers. "One on my phone too. I hope Dad's okay?"

"Ring her back, will you, my cord's too short and I've only got twelve per cent."

"I'll FaceTime her, shall I?" The call rang several times and then connected, but all they could see was what appeared to be Doreen's left nostril.

"Mum, move the phone away a bit, will you?" Jo said over Bobbi's shoulder. Doreen came into focus, her face perfectly made up and hair done despite the fact it was only eight in the morning there.

"Oh, there you girls are," she said.

"Is everything okay?" Bobbi asked. "We saw you've been ringing."

"Oh yes, I just wanted to make sure you got on the plane all right. And I was thinking you could get me a bottle of that Mambo Number Five perfume at the airport."

"Chanel," Bobbi whispered at Jo's baffled face.

"Maybe we can pick some up on the way home, Mum, we're already in London now."

"Oh well, don't forget to get me something nice at Harrods, won't you?" she reminded them. Again. "Bobbi, you look terrible. Have you brushed your hair?"

"We've just got here, Mum—" Jo started to say, but Doreen cut her off.

"I've had a terrible night's sleep. I was awake most of the night. I heard the clock strike midnight, and one and two."

"You could turn off the chimes," Bobbi said.

"Well, anyway, I had to get up and take half a sleeping pill in the end. And I've got golf this afternoon and I need to take a plate."

There was a pause. Bobbi and Jo stayed silent. Doreen opened her mouth.

"I suppose I could make my ..."

"Actually, Mum, we'd better go," Jo said. "We're a bit shattered and we want to get an early night before the show tomorrow."

"Oh yes, that Harry Belafonte. I hope you enjoy it. You never know, you might get his autograph," Doreen said.

Jo snorted as they heard their father singing from behind Doreen, "*Day, is a day-o. Daylight come and we want go home,*" and Bobbi took the opportunity to say a quick goodbye and hang up.

"Harry Belafonte?" she laughed.

"Is he even still alive?" Jo asked, still grinning as she headed off to the shower, flinging her hairbrush out to Jo as she shut the door.

◇

They'd dressed in warm, clean clothes and, grumbling a bit, Bobbi had followed Jo out for a 'brisk walk and some fresh air'. Brisk walking wasn't Bobbi's thing, Jo knew, but she'd read a bit about staving off jet lag and swore that this was one of the best things for it.

Luckily they'd found a pub about 200 metres from the hotel and popped in for a quick drink and a bite to eat, so the

walk was brisk and short. Jo had an instant sense of wellbe-
ing. Almost every British pub she'd ever been in was just like
any other British pub she'd ever been in; cosy and friendly.

Bobbi studied a row of antique chamber pots hanging
above the fireplace while they waited for their meals to
arrive.

"We should get one of those for Mum," she said, with a
glint in her eye. "If we put a plant in it, she might not even
realise what it was. Tell her it was from Harrods."

Jo snorted loudly at the thought. "It could come in useful
during the trip too. Like if you wanted a wee or I needed to
barf in it."

"Both possibilities."

"Maybe we should have thought of carrying some kind of
vessel around with us before now. Would you tie it to the
handle of your suitcase or wear it as a hat?"

Jo laughed loudly at the thought. "It's not even that funny," she said. "We must be jet lagged."

They ate their cheese soufflés and headed back to the hotel for an early night.

"Airplanes always make me so gassy," Jo complained as
they lay in their beds.

"Everything makes you gassy," Bobbi replied. "But I'm
glad for the single beds at this point so I don't have to feel
you farting, even if I can still hear you."

Jo laughed. "But my bed is lovely and warm now."

"Ewww, I don't even want to think about that. This room

is tiny though. I hope we're not crammed into rooms like this the whole time." Bobbi yawned loudly and rolled over.

"That reminds me, I've found the cutest little B&B for us to stay in tomorrow," Jo said cheerfully.

CHAPTER 6

Bobbi

It had been a long day after waking up too early that morning, slightly jet lagged. They'd gone down to Neal's Yard early for coffee and a coconut cream pie, Jo complaining that Uncle Bill weighed a ton in her day pack.

"I told you to leave him behind in the hotel," Bobbi said again, "but you insisted he come with us, so you're carrying him."

They'd then done a walking tour called Grime and Punishment. Their tour guide Jesse had been a great guy, very knowledgeable, and equally as funny. It had a less touristy feel than a lot of tours, and both Bobbi and Jo had been intrigued by the story of the great London beer flood in 1814, where a huge three-storey vat of beer had burst, killing six people. Unreal. Bobbi would have to tell Dad all about that one. It also had gruesome bits and sleazy bits, which was just the sort of stuff Bobbi and Jo loved.

◇

They caught the train to Birmingham that afternoon. Bobbi was already over carting cutout Bayley around and after stuffing her in yet another cab, was looking forward to ditching her after the show that night.

"This place is a horror story," hissed Bobbi as they walked up the stairs to their room.

"Shhh, she'll hear you," Jo whispered back, "and it's not *that* bad."

"Jo, there's a stuffed rat on the windowsill, and I'm pretty sure that's a real donkey head over the fireplace. We are *not* staying here."

The proprietor was a tiny hunched woman in her sixties called Jolene. She put a key into the door at the end of the corridor. "I have to say, I was surprised to see you were ladies. I'd assumed by the names that you were two men. Still, I'm sure you'll feel most welcome in the Elton suite. More towels are in the wardrobe if you need them, and breakfast will be served at seven in the Dollhouse Room. Let me know if you need anything else."

She opened the door with a flourish, gave Bobbi the key, and scuttled down the hall.

"Holy Rocket Man!" Bobbi choked back a demented laugh as she walked in. The Elton suite was a mismatched tribute to Elton John himself and where the sequins stopped, the rainbows began. The bed was a shape that she assumed was supposed to be a grand piano. The linen was bedazzled in a blinding array of multi-coloured sequins and ruffles. A mural on the wall behind the pink satin headboard showed Elton, resplendent in white feathers and red glasses, larger than life, petting a peacock.

"I'll have to take some photos for the girls back at the bar. They'll be green with envy. We are *so* staying here."

Jo had gone quiet and was staring in horror at the decor. "Do you think they shoot porn in here?"

Hysterical laughter bubbled up as Bobbi poked her head into the bathroom.

On the gold vanity was a welcome pack with, amongst the regular toiletries, a rainbow tube of lube and a packet of flavoured condoms.

"I see what she was referring to now when she mentioned thinking we were blokes."

"What?" asked Jo, picking up a bejewelled cigar box and turning it over in her hands, before replacing it carefully back on the coffee table. "What do you mean?"

"She thinks we're a couple," Bobbi snorted. "Ohh, let's give her a thrill." She leapt onto the admittedly very comfy bed and started to jump up and down, making the bedhead bang against the peacock.

"Cut it out," hissed Jo, laughing.

Bobbi faked a loud moan and cried out, "Yeah, right there, babe."

Jo jumped on her and tried to cover her mouth with her palm, the bed squeaking and the headboard banging even more as they wrestled, but ended up shrieking with laughter when Bobbi licked her. "That's disgusting, Bob, no licking."

"What sort of lesbian would I be if I didn't lick?"

They lay on the bed snorting and occasionally fake moaning until Bobbi said, "Imagine if we had one of those DNA torches," which made them both leap off and fight to get in the bathroom door first to shower. Bobbi won, but only because she laughed so hard she'd done a little pee in her pants.

◇

"What are you planning to wear to this thing?" Bobbi asked Jo. "I feel like nothing I've packed is quite cool enough."

"Actually," Jo looked a bit sheepish, "I ordered some T-shirts online before we left."

She pulled out the matching tops and held one up to her chest. 'TREAT PEOPLE WITH KINDNESS' was written across it in a rainbow-coloured text.

"You can't be serious," Bobbi said. "No way."

"Come on, Bob," Jo pleaded, "I'm trying to be as visible as possible, for maximum impact. It's Harry's catchphrase."

"Bloody hell," Bobbi grumbled, "the things I do for you and Bay."

CHAPTER 7

Jo

"This writing is a bit stretched. It makes my boobs look massive," Bobbi complained, tugging the T-shirt down over her jeans. "And pink is not a good colour with my hair. I look like Ronald fucking McDonald."

Her wine glass was perched precariously on the bathroom vanity as she combed furiously at her unruly curls, dyed her signature cherry red. Jo itched to get up and move it, fearing it was going to clatter onto the floor and smash. The neon pink of the T-shirt did indeed clash but that was kind of the point of standing out in a crowd.

"See and be seen," she replied and shovelled a cracker loaded with cheese and cranberry paste into her mouth. "Now let's go see Harry."

◇

Downstairs Jo rang the bell at the small front desk to summon Jolene, who looked rather bewildered to see them in their matching T-shirts and even more puzzled that they were carrying the cardboard cutout. She kept opening and shutting her mouth while glancing between them all.

"We need to get to the Utilita Arena, Jolene. Are we best to go to the New Street Station and walk from there?"

"Er — yes, yes, or there is a bus. But it's quite a short walk from the station." Jolene looked uncertainly at Bayley. Who knew what was going through her head.

"Thank you, Jolene. Have a nice evening," Jo replied politely.

Jolene just gave them a brief nod in response.

"And treat people with kindness," Bobbi added, slapping Jo on the arse for effect as they left.

◇

"Follow that group in the 'Adore You' T-shirts," Jo whispered as they exited the station, and they joined the procession, mostly female, headed towards the arena.

Bayley's head hit a girl in the back as Jo swung her from under her right arm to her left. "Oops, sorry."

The girl turned around, her eyes widening as she took in the two middle-aged women with the bikini-clad Bayley.

"Oh, that's totally okay. Who is that, like, your daughter? That's so nice of you to bring her. Is she—"

At that moment there was a loud shriek ahead in the milling crowd and everyone craned their necks to see what was happening or what they were missing, but it turned out that the long, black car that had slithered passed merely contained a grey-haired man in a suit, probably a Birmingham resident on his way to a business dinner.

The queue when they reached the arena snaked some way in front of them and Jo leant against the guard fence ready for a bit of a wait.

"Sometimes I wish I still smoked. We should have brought a hip flask of vodka," Bobbi complained. They'd already downed a bottle of wine before they'd left the B&B.

"Straight vodka," Jo mused.

"No, gay," Bobbi replied and they both cackled. The Harry quotes and jokes were getting more and more regular since they'd arrived.

"I hope there's some interesting banter between Harry and the audience tonight," Bobbi said enthusiastically.

"Yeah, and hopefully he notices Bayley." She shoved Bayley at Bobbi. "Here, you can hold her for a bit. I don't know why I have to be the one to lug her around."

Bobbi took the cutout and draped an arm over one thin shoulder.

"Oh, my god, I'm so excited! I can't believe that in such a short time I'm going to actually get to see Harry Styles in person, in real life," a young girl in front of them gushed to her friend. "I just know I'm going to cry."

"I'll probably faint," her friend added. "I feel like I might faint right now. I haven't eaten anything since breakfast." Jo was very concerned to hear this and tapped the girl on the shoulder.

"You really shouldn't do that. Here," she rustled around in her shoulder bag and pulled out a granola bar, "have this. Have you got some water? You don't want to get dehydrated. The last thing you want is to pass out and miss the whole show."

"She's right, ya know, Chloe," the girl next to her said bossily, and Chloe hesitantly took the bar and then ripped it open.

"Thank you so much, that's really nice."

"How about you?" Jo asked her friend. "Have you eaten? You girls need to take better care of yourselves."

The friend shook her head. "I'm okay, my mam made me have my tea before she'd let me come out."

"Anyone else?" Jo called, brandishing the box of granola bars in the air.

"I wouldn't mind one, if that's okay," a blonde girl wearing a pair of red heart-shaped sunglasses replied. "I haven't eaten either, I just couldn't. I thought I might puke."

"Is that your daughter?" Chloe asked shyly, indicating Bayley. "I like her watermelon bikini, it's soooo cute."

"Thanks, sweetheart. She didn't make it so we're taking her with us to see Harry," Jo said, surprised when Chloe hugged her, and said she thought she was a lovely mum.

"I'd love it if my mum did that for me," she said a little tearily.

"I can barely stand this. I think I *am* going to puke," Heart-sunglasses moaned.

"I think we should have a sing-a-long," Bobbi said quickly. "What's your favourite Harry song? Let's do 'Sweet Creature'."

To Jo's surprise Bobbi broke into song and all around her dozens of girls joined in, and one very sweet male voice from right behind them.

"Now 'What Makes You Beautiful'," someone in front of them shouted. Everyone cheered. Bobbi joined in with abandon and Jo looked at her narrowly.

"I can't believe you know all the words."

Her sister flipped her the middle finger and then turned to the young man behind them. "You have a really lovely singing voice, you know. What's your name?"

"Oh, well, ta, I'm Adam. I think it's lovely you ladies have brought your daughter to see Harry."

"She's Jo's daughter. My niece Bayley," Bobbi told him. "I'm Bobbi."

Adam politely held out a hand to Bobbi and she shook it. "Are you here with friends?"

"Just on my own," Adam told her. "I think Harry's amazing. I'd like to sing, myself. I'm actually going to most of his UK shows on this tour."

Jo turned and beamed at Adam. "Oh, us too. We're off to

Manchester after this."

Bobbi's eyebrows shot up and then she narrowed her eyes at her sister suspiciously. "We're what?"

"Not all of them," Jo mumbled, "I couldn't get tickets to Sheffield. I ruled out Dublin too, being, you know, a plane ride away."

Bobbi was frowning, one eyebrow raised.

"I think you were right, we should have brought our jackets," Jo said quickly, rubbing her bare arms.

"Don't try to change the subject, Josie. How did this 'us too' happen?"

"Um, I'd had a few drinks when I bought the tickets. I didn't realise until the next day how many I'd bought."

"Fucking hell," Bobbi muttered.

"So, your daughter," Adam interjected, as if sensing a wee bit of tension between them. "Was she a big fan?"

Jo was relieved that he'd changed the subject. "I wouldn't say she's a fan as such, but there's certainly something about Harry. He seems to be so kind and just gentle and thoughtful. I'm sure if they could meet—"

"Oh. I thought maybe you were bringing her because she was ... well, anyway, she's gorgeous," Adam replied, and Jo beamed at him. "You'll have to go to the door on the other side of the arena after the show. I've heard that that's where he'll come out when he leaves. I'm sure if he sees Bayley he'll want to know your story. It's pretty ... er ... unique."

"Thanks, Adam," Jo smiled. "Your accent — are you

Scottish?"

"Aye."

The line had started to move and Bobbi and Jo, being seated in a different section to Adam, who was headed to the mosh pit, waved him off as they were directed to the correct entrance.

◇

"At least we have seats," Bobbi sighed as she sat, grappling with the two bottles of cider she'd purchased, as well as Bayley.

"Careful, don't put Bay down there, there's a puddle of something. Who knows what it might be."

Bobbi propped Bayley awkwardly against the seats in front of them. Jo wondered how she'd break it to Bobbi that the rest of their tickets weren't seated.

If the people behind them were surprised to see a full-sized cutout, or annoyed that she might block their view, they didn't show it. Plenty of people around them had signs and flags, some of them quite large.

Bobbi peered dubiously at the stage. "I'm not sure Harry's going to see Bay from down there, Jo."

"We'll have to hope we get to meet him at the end then. See if you can come up with a good line, Bob, for when he talks to us. You're much better at that kind of thing than I am."

The arena was packed with excited and overheated bodies. Jo was, she had to admit, feeling quite excited herself now.

She huffed and tried to blow her sticky fringe from her face.

Bobbi glanced over at her. "Please tell me you're not going to cry or faint or anything stupid like that?" The opening act had finished and the lights dimmed and dramatic music started, proclaiming the start of the show. Jo was, thankfully, saved from answering. She wasn't entirely convinced that she wouldn't start crying.

◇

Afterwards she decided she needn't have worried about not having seated tickets for the remaining three concerts. She and Bobbi had spent most of the time on their feet waving Bayley around, shrieking, singing and dancing, along with everyone around them.

"You knew almost all the words to all of the songs," she accused Bobbi suspiciously as they made their way slowly out of the arena.

Bobbi gave her a wry look. "Well, all those links you sent — it's like I've been brainwashed, thanks to you."

"Wouldn't be hard to do," Jo said under her breath and then laughed when Bobbi whacked her.

CHAPTER 8

Bobbi

Bobbi had to admit, Harry was one hell of a performer and his band were awesome. The show had been spectacular. That boy had something undefinable that just gave him an edge. She thought maybe she was halfway in love with him. Oh, to be twenty years younger. She wasn't even that bothered now to be standing around waiting with Adam, who they'd met up with again, on the off chance of spotting Harry as he left the arena. Not to mention, the eye candy was fantastic. One of Harry's security detail was leaning against the door, watching the small crowd. He was smoking hot; he had to be at least six foot five, and he had muscles on his muscles. He had one of those gruff, serious faces like he never smiled. Maybe ex-army? Bobbi could imagine he'd have no trouble lifting a woman up and—

"Bobbi, do you think she's all right?" Jo pointed to one of

the girls from earlier whose friends were all gathered around her and sounding a bit panicked.

"Here, Adam, would you mind holding Bayley while we check she's okay?" Bobbi passed the cutout over to Adam and she and Jo went over to see if they could help.

Millie, it turned out, was diabetic and her blood sugars had dropped. Bobbi and Jo took her to get something to eat and then eventually got her and her friend into an Uber and finally they headed back to the arena doors, but it had taken more time than they'd realised and they found everyone but a few straggling concertgoers and the security guy had left.

"Shit," Jo said "Bayley."

She rushed up to the guard and started to ask him if he had seen her. Bobbi dragged behind her. Her feet were starting to ache in her high-heeled boots, and she needed to pee.

The security guy had a concerned look on his face.

"So, Jo, was it? You've lost your daughter? What does she look like?"

"She's gorgeous, blonde, shoulder-length hair. Probably a bit too skinny in my opinion ..."

"Okay, so what was she wearing? How tall?"

"She's in a red bikini and she's life-size."

The guy had an incredulous look on his face. "What the hell, she's in a bikini? In this weather? Why the hell is she wearing a bikini? And what does life-size mean?"

There was a moment of realisation on his face as he looked up and saw Bobbi as she caught up to them. "Oh, the cutout weirdos," he nodded as if he recalled seeing them before. "And what about you, Red? I suppose you lost your kid as well?"

Bobbi felt a little sick. The smile slid off her face. She'd lost her baby years ago, but sometimes it still felt raw.

"Listen, Andre, I may have contemplated climbing you like a tree earlier, but you're as big of an arsehole as you are hot. Inconceivable."

She stormed off, forcing Jo to follow. The security guard watched them go, looking bemused.

"The hot ones are always crackers," he said under his breath.

◇

Breakfast the next morning was a strange affair. Jolene kept bringing out little dishes with various offerings, lifting the cloches with a flourish, then hovering until the table had eaten them before swooping in to clear. They'd had Bircher muesli, a fruit plate, corn muffins and now pigs in blankets. There was no polite way of turning anything down and the food combination, along with the row of creepy dolls staring at them from the windowsill of the 'Dollhouse Room', was making Bobbi feel a little queasy.

The B&B had been a bad choice. The bed was comfy, but the water pipes were noisy and the water took ages to heat up. It was an old house and the heater was set way too low. They'd had to heap on four sparkly-coloured blankets in the night. The traffic sounds had been constant and far too early that morning they'd been woken up by the rubbish truck banging bin lids outside their window.

Jolene also only had herbal tea, no coffee. A final straw of sorts to Bobbi's mind.

She made polite conversation with the older couple to her right and discovered they were both retired doctors from France. She hoped Jo wouldn't ask them for any gory work stories. She had a weird fascination with that stuff, and her bizarre medical trivia knowledge was scary. Bobbi's stomach lurched at the thought.

They were talking about their parents, when Jolene suddenly dropped the bowl of baked beans she was holding onto Bobbi's plate, splattering her and the tablecloth with red sauce.

"You're sisters?" There was an awkward silence.

"Ah, yes?" Jo questioned, looking puzzled. "Is there a problem?"

"I do my best to run an open-minded establishment, even if I don't personally approve of my guests' lifestyle choices, but I will not condone that kind of filthy behaviour. You will have to leave at once. You're disgusting!" Jolene shouted. "Get out."

Bobbi glanced at Jo, who was looking as puzzled as she felt. She had her mouth open and her fork was paused halfway to her mouth. The other guests around the table seemed to be equally lost at the path this turn of events had taken as well, she noticed.

"There must be some sort of mistake," Bobbi tried saying, but Jolene was pulling Jo up from her chair by her arm and shooing her out of the room. She was muttering something that sounded like a prayer, and hissed over her shoulder, "Be gone with you, sinners. Out, out!"

It struck Bobbi then, as she followed Jo from the room, that perhaps Jolene had heard them pretending to get it on the day before. Should she explain that they weren't having an incestuous relationship? Probably, but she couldn't really see the point. They had planned to leave after breakfast anyway. Neither of them wanted to ever spend another night there. Jolene probably had a glass to the door. Really, it wasn't that funny, and rather embarrassing, but awkward situations always made Bobbi laugh and she kept snorting as she tried to hold it together.

She followed Jo up the stairs and into the room to collect their bags.

"What the heck?" Jo asked, turning to Bobbi as she shut the door behind them. "What was that all about?"

Bobbi explained her theory and Jo blanched. "Oh, my God. Should we say something to her?"

"Nah, what's the point? Let her stew about it, she's a nutter anyway. And think of the fun we can have with the Trip Advisor review."

Bobbi went into the en suite to pack their toiletries while Jo made sure they had everything from the room. While she was in the bathroom, Bobbi also swiped the condoms and lube. Just in case.

They dragged their bags down the hallway, passing Jolene, who stood with her lips pursed, holding the door open for them. Bobbi leant over and whispered, "Love thine brother, Jolene."

◇

Jo was still too quiet three hours later. Bobbi wasn't sure if she was just tired, or mad. It was too damned cold to be outside, so after they'd frozen themselves solid at a museum with an 1850s replica ironworks town, the warmth inside the Prince of Wales pub was heavenly. Bobbi was finally starting to thaw when Jo blurted out, "This is your fault, Bobbi, if you hadn't made out like we were having furious lesbo sex..."

Bobbi laughed so hard it made her snort her mulled wine out her nose.

"What the hell is furious lesbo sex? My mind boggles."

Jo looked like she was trying not to smile. Bobbi knew she could never stay angry for long.

"Come on," said Bobbi, "it was funny. You're just upset that we lost Bayley and the chance to marry Harry off to her. I'm sure we'll think of another plan for the next show."

"True," Jo said grudgingly. "It was a great show though, wasn't it?"

Bobbi had to admit, it had been fantastic. Better even than Prince when she saw him in Auckland a few years ago, just before he'd died. She was looking forward to seeing Harry perform again. And to see what he wore. Last night's suit was glorious. Even if that hulking great bodyguard had been a bit of a wanker, she still wouldn't mind a chance to ogle his arse. Her mind began to wander ...

"Anyway, can we at least ditch the cheesy T-shirts next time and go looking hot? On both levels? Long-sleeved *and* sexy. Oh, and we have to go to the Cadbury factory too, if we've got time."

Jo looked at her scathingly. "Well, duh. Chocolate. That's a no-brainer."

CHAPTER 9

Adam

Adam was somewhat regretting his decision now. It had seemed kind of noble, or at least amusing to continue the quest to get Bayley to Harry. And Jo and Bobbi had been kinda cool for old ladies. But he was drawing a lot of attention carrying around a cutout of a chick under his arm. Attention he really didn't want.

The cutout had been a handy distraction last night when he'd turned up at his sister's flat looking for a place to crash. Hannah lived with two girls she'd met in the dorms her first year. She was doing a business degree and had been studying when he turned up, hoping to crash on her couch. They didn't see each other so much now, especially since their mam died and they weren't living in the same house any more, but she'd seemed happy to see him. He said he'd gotten permission to leave school for a night to go to a concert.

That wasn't quite the truth and he didn't tell her he wasn't planning on going back either. She'd tell their da for sure.

He wasn't going to leave 'cause he hated school or anything. He just didn't think it mattered all that much if he passed the year. He wasn't going to use any of it to become a musician. And plenty of successful people left school early. But he wasn't sure his da would agree.

As a bonus, after seeing him carrying Bayley, he was pretty sure his sister was convinced now that he was straight. She'd been asking lots of questions since he'd been boarding in London about who he fancied. It wasn't that he was ashamed of being gay. He wasn't. He just didn't want to tell people yet. He hadn't even had a chance to *do* anything gay yet. To prove it for sure to himself. I mean, it's not like he'd ever fancied any girls. Not even a looker like Bayley, and he definitely fancied Harry. And Thomas.

He didn't want to think too much about Thomas. Thomas made him feel all butterflies and sweaty. Thomas was the main thing he'd miss about not being at school any more.

He was kinda regretting not asking him to the concert last night. It was awesome, and Harry was so talented, so he'd had a brilliant time. He'd probably have enjoyed it twice as much if Thomas had been there.

If only it hadn't meant everyone at school knowing they'd gone. Thomas was already 'out' and so that would be an instant rainbow flag on his head.

But he felt like a coward now. He'd have to come out

sometime. Still, he had the two tickets to the London show so there was still time to pluck up the nerve to ask him. If the school didn't get wind of the fact he wasn't back home in Scotland at his grandmother's funeral.

He didn't really care if the school expelled him or whatever, but he was worried what would happen if his da found out. He'd be pissed. But Adam couldn't see the point of doing his A levels. He wanted to be a musician, not an accountant. His father wasn't the easiest person to talk to about that sort of stuff. It had gotten harder after his mam had died and now he was away at school, things seemed even worse.

He leant Bayley against the station wall, put in his earbuds and waited for the train to Manchester while he daydreamed about making it big like Harry.

CHAPTER 10

Jo

"Mum? I can just see the top of your head, move your screen. Mother? Have you got your microphone turned on? Oh, that's better."

Jo gave a little wave as her daughter came into view on the iPad screen.

"Where the hell are you? It looks like you're on a bus."

"We're on a train. On the way to Manchester. I thought I'd just give you a quick call before we get going."

"It's after midnight here. Did you not consider I might be asleep?"

"Oh, sorry, sweetheart, did I wake you?" Jo hadn't even thought about the time difference before she'd FaceTimed.

Bayley tucked a loose strand of hair behind her ear. She didn't look at all tired even though she must have finished a shift in the restaurant earlier. In fact her cheeks were pink and she looked as though she were thriving in the new job.

"No, it's okay, Sam and I are just chilling and watching *Dunkirk*."

Bobbi leant over so her face was partially in the shot.

"How's it going, Bay?"

Bayley grinned. "Everything's great. You guys look like you've been having fun — oh, hang on a sec, here's Sam, he wants to say hi."

She got up from where she'd been sitting in the armchair and took her laptop over to Bobbi's leopard print sofa where Sam was lounging, legs outstretched, wrapped in a fuzzy pink blanket. There was an open packet of digestive biscuits beside him. Bayley picked up Sam's legs and slid underneath them, plonking his feet back into her lap. She turned the laptop so he could talk to Bobbi.

"Hey, Sam, how's my bar?"

"It's all good. There was a leak in the bar fridge but nothing major. All sorted now. Bay and I make a great team, we don't even need you here, Bob. Just sign the deed for the bar over to me now if you like," he grinned widely.

"Tempting."

Sam's face disappeared and Bayley came back into view. Jo resisted the urge to do that 'mum' thing and tell her that several of the buttons were undone on her top and she could see practically down to her navel. She wouldn't have wanted to embarrass her in front of Sam and draw attention to that.

"We've been trying out a couple of new recipes for the bar

snacks and the pretzels have definitely been a big hit. Gary's going to put them on permanently."

Jo knew the pretzels had been Bayley's idea. She'd be happy Bobbi's head chef was listening to her suggestions. She described the dip she'd perfected for them, a mayonnaise with mustard and rosemary.

"Great decision," Bobbi told her. "How is Gary getting on with finding a supplier for—"

Jo just happened to glance out the window at that moment and let out a gasp.

"Bay, we've got to go," she interrupted. "We'll talk later. Don't stay up too late. Bye, Sam."

"Mother, I'm—"

But Jo disconnected before she could finish.

"Jo, what the hell?" Bobbi was looking at her like she'd gone nuts.

She pointed out the window. "It's Bayley."

Bobbi leant over her just in time for them to see the bottom half of Bayley disappearing into a carriage two down from them.

"How the — what is Bayley doing on the train to Manchester? Stay here while I investigate." Bobbi stood and hurried to the end of the carriage where she disappeared. A few minutes later she came back, Adam in tow, carrying Bayley, who was looking a little more battered than she had been when they'd started out. He seemed pleased to see them.

"I'm so stoked I found you. I wasn't looking forward to

dragging your daughter round till the concert. She's giving me too much unwelcome attention." He shoved his duffel bag onto the overhead rack above the seat.

There was nowhere really for Bayley to go so they put her on the window seat next to Adam. She gazed blankly out onto the tracks. Adam unwound his scarf and wrapped it gently around Bayley's neck before flopping down into his seat. Jo was unsure whether he thought she was cold or was trying to protect her modesty. A bikini probably wasn't the usual attire on an intercity train trip in spring. Or any time really.

"Second time lucky, Bayley. Tomorrow night could be your night," Adam told Bayley's unblinking face.

He turned to Jo and Bobbi. "Have you been to Manchester before?"

"No, and we need to find somewhere to stay," Jo replied. "Where would be good?"

Adam shifted in his seat. "I don't really know Manchester. I'm probably just sleeping outside the arena somewhere. I'm guessing you're probably more into a comfortable bed."

Jo gasped in horror. "Why are you sleeping outside? It's way too cold for that."

There was a pause. "I'm kind of too young to stay in a hostel. I'm not eighteen yet."

Bobbi frowned at Adam. "Well, that's it. You're not sleeping outside. You can stay with us. Or we can come to a hostel with you. We'll say you're our nephew or something."

"Would you do that?" He seemed relieved. It looked like it was going to rain.

The train started then and they settled back in their seats. Adam put his earbuds in and closed his eyes and Jo pulled a battered paperback from her handbag. There was a bookmark about a quarter of the way in. She opened it and sighed heavily.

"So, *Dunkirk*, huh?"

Jo looked up and saw that Bobbi was smirking at her. "I know. Obviously a Harry fan after all. I knew she was just pretending she wasn't that interested."

Bobbi considered for a minute. "Either that or it was Sam's choice. Although I thought they were more into romcoms. Except Bayley does say she only ever agrees to watch *The Princess Bride* with me out of sheer devotion."

"You've seen that movie so many times. Everyone else has gotten sick of watching with you."

"It's a classic. Bayley secretly loves it as much as me. What's not to love? You just have no class."

It started to rain then, obscuring the view and Jo sighed contentedly. "I do love a train trip."

Bobbi agreed. "It's certainly less stressful than you being a Nervous Nelly, crawling around in a rental car."

"Or having to deal with your terrible navigational skills," Jo replied tartly. "Remember when we missed our flight from Christchurch that time because you told me we were heading north when we were really going west?"

Bobbi huffed. "We never would have found that great bakery with the lamb shank pies if we hadn't though, would we?"

"That's true," Jo conceded.

A conductor came past at that moment. He looked pointedly at the cutout of Bayley and shook his head. "Been in this job for thirty years," he muttered and quickly checked Adam's ticket and moved on without another word.

Adam tucked his ticket back into his pocket and gave them a cheeky grin. "Wonder what scenario he was imagining." He replaced his earbud and went back to his music.

◇

The rain was steady outside. It hadn't really stopped drizzling since they'd arrived in Manchester late that afternoon. Jo plucked a spicy cauliflower wing from the sharing platter and chewed it with satisfaction. The food was delectable. She'd taken a photo and sent it in a message to Bayley.

A gas fire warmed the crowded pub. The only people outside in the garden bar were a young couple huddled under the overhang holding hands and smoking.

"I can't believe Adam's parents would let him wander around all over the place like he is. He seems so young, even for seventeen. I'd never have let Bay go off like that at that age, no accommodation booked or anything. What kind of people are they?"

Bobbi looked up from her iPad and stirred her vodka with the paper straw, which was now looking rather limp and soggy. "I know. I was just thinking about how he'd been planning on sleeping outside in the rain tonight. If you'd let Bayley do something like that, I'd probably have killed you."

Jo laughed. "No, you wouldn't, you'd have offered to go along with her, and paid for all the hotels too."

Bobbi grinned. "You're probably right."

They had left Adam at the hostel, playing cards with a couple of young football fans from Argentina and eating pot noodles. He'd seemed happy enough and hadn't wanted to come out for something to eat.

◇

It had been a little trickier finding somewhere to stay than they'd anticipated and they'd had to settle for two beds in a mixed room of four for Bobbi and herself and a bed in a male dorm for Adam. To their dismay, backpacks lay on both the single beds in the room and they had been left with the bunk. They hadn't yet resolved who had to have the top — though Bobbi was insisting that after their supposed lesbian sex encounter in the Elton room, she was definitely a bottom.

"Do lesbians have tops and bottoms?" Jo had asked doubtfully. "Because there's no way you'd be submissive, Bob. I'm way more likely to be the bottom." She was eyeing the steep ladder to the top bunk dubiously.

Their roommates still hadn't materialised by the time they'd showered in the slightly grimy shared bathroom and donned raincoats to venture out to a nearby restaurant.

Hence, Bobbi was now googling their accommodation for the following night and for Glasgow in two days' time. They probably should have looked at this earlier. Harry was a very popular boy, it seemed.

They'd left their bags, which thankfully locked, and Bayley, leaning up next to the bunk in their dorm to keep guard, and headed out to dinner.

◇

As Jo sipped her drink, she wondered what would happen if they needed to get up to pee in the night. They'd have to make sure they didn't have too much to drink.

Bobbi raised her glass. "Bottoms up."

CHAPTER 11

Bobbi

"Ohh look, cocktails," said Bobbi as they walked past another bar on the way home. There were a few 'specials' advertised on a blackboard outside and they all sounded pretty good.

"Shall we?"

"Maybe just one or two," agreed Jo.

Seating themselves at the bar, they ordered two Rosebuds, and got talking with a couple who were celebrating their third wedding anniversary. They had heard their accents and wanted to know if they were Australian.

As they were sitting discussing Canadian versus American accents and New Zealand versus Australian, a large group pushed through the doors cackling and shrieking. There was a lot of pink, and a lot of penis everywhere.

"Oh man, I hate hens' nights," Bobbi groaned.

"Oh, let them enjoy it. It looks fun. I wish I'd done it when I got married."

One of the women, with a sash reading 'Maid of Dishonour', overheard, turning to them from the bar, where she was ordering shots.

"Didja not have a hens' night?" she asked, slurring slightly. She threw her arm around Jo's shoulder and leant heavily against her. "You have to come out on the lash with us then."

She called over her shoulder to another girl who was wearing what looked to be a large condom hat on her head. "Jen, can you giz us a hand with the tray, yeah?"

Jen wiggled her way through and slid the tray of shots off the bar with one hand, holding it precariously over Bobbi's head for a few seconds, before shuffling back through the crowd. Miss Dishonour was pulling Jo by the hand over to a booth, so Bobbi said her goodbyes to the guys, and tottered after them.

There were two older women in the booth, and two girls who looked barely old enough to drink. The rest of the wedding party were gathered around Jen taking shots off the tray.

"I got you a vodka 'n' soda," said the woman to one of the older ladies as she motioned Jo to sit down next to her. "Sorry, what was your name?" she asked Jo.

Before Jo could reply she was talking again. "This lady was saying, she never had a hens', so I told her to join us, right? More the merrier 'n' all that."

There was a loud toast of "To being more the merrier," and they all downed their shots.

One of the ladies offered to get another tray of shots and headed back to the bar.

"So, I'm Jo, and this is my sister Bobbi. Who's the lucky bride then?"

The youngest-looking girl pointed into the group at a blonde wearing a tiara and pink veil. "Madeline," she said in a bored tone. "The ugly one with the big nose."

Madeline looked over at her and gave her the finger. "Mam," she whined, "can't these two go home now?"

The lady next to Jo smiled indulgently at Madeline and the teen. "Carrie-Ann, be nice. This is your sister's night. And Madeline, I told your dad to pick them up at eleven, so quit going on." She turned and smiled. "I'm Teressa, and that's my youngest, Carrie-Ann. That's her mate Leah," she indicated the other girl and then the woman next to her "and this is Gail. She's the mother of Donny — the groom-to-be."

Gail gave them both a tight-lipped smile. She didn't look like she was enjoying herself much. "I'll order us some more cocktails," Bobbi told Jo. Teressa's vodka soda was still half full, but Gail didn't have a drink. "Can I get you something?" Bobbi asked her. Gail sniffed. "Nice of *someone* to ask," she said sourly, "but I'm not drinking tonight . Someone has to stay sober to make sure things don't get out of hand with this lot."

"Right," said Bobbi as Teressa rolled her eyes, "something

non-alcoholic then maybe?"

"Lemon, lime and bitters," Gail replied tightly.

Carrie-Ann and Leah slid out of the booth to use the loos. Two of the girls sat down in their place.

"Y'all right?" said a dark-haired girl with long false eyelashes. "I'm Katie, this is Leticia." The redhead next to her waved and looked nervously over at Gail as if she were going to write notes on their behaviour and print up a report in the morning.

◇

When Bobbi got back with the drinks, she'd also paid for another round of shots for the group that was met with loud applause.

Jo gave her a brief rundown on what she'd missed as she sat down in the booth.

"So Madeline and Donny have only been going out for six months. Donny used to date Cara," she said, pointing to a short, slightly plump girl with a sash saying 'Bad Influence'. She was leaning against the wall, checking her phone.

"And Raya, she's the one who invited us over, is with Donny's best mate Steve."

Raya was currently leaning on Jen and talking animatedly with Madeline who was sucking on her drink through a penis straw and nodding earnestly.

"And," Jo continued, like she was telling Bobbi what she'd missed on an episode of a soap opera, "Jen, who's Madeline's cousin, is single at the moment." Jo finished off her cocktail and set the glass down before continuing. "She was dating Landon, but he cheated on her with Nina and Nina had to be taken out of the wedding party." She paused and then added, "She was a bridesmaid."

Bobbi grinned at Jo and handed her a drink. "Cheers," she said, "here's to the days of our lives." There was no way she was going to remember all these names.

"Where's my penis straw?" Jo grumbled.

◇

"I love hens' parties," Bobbi proclaimed four drinks and two shots later. The two younger girls had been picked up and Teressa had let her hair down. Literally. It kept flicking in Bobbi's face as they shimmied and shook on the dance floor.

Even Gail seemed to be having a good time and was now wearing a sign saying 'Don't kiss the bride; kiss me'. Admittedly, it was on her back and Bobbi wasn't sure she knew it was there, but still. She seemed to be more relaxed and was currently chatting to a group of businessmen in suits, along with Jen and Raya. Bobbi could hear her laughing. She sounded startlingly like the penguin in the old Batman series.

They'd moved on to a new bar, where there was a dance floor. There was also karaoke. Jo had made Bobbi promise, when they'd got there, that they would under no circumstances get up and sing. It had happened before once on a cruise and the only reason people kept requesting them was because they were so awful it was entertaining.

Raya stood up on a bar stool to gather them up for another round of shots. One of the businessmen was shouting, she told them, and they all toasted with "Here's to Dave" before knocking them back.

"Jen is being very thankful to Dave," Jo whispered as she nudged Bobbi and angled her head to the pair as they wandered to the back of the club, his hand inching down to rest on her arse, hers in his back pocket. They disappeared into the disabled toilet after a furtive look around.

"Jesus," Bobbi frowned, "that was fast."

They went over to the bar for another look at the drinks list.

"We have to remember to have water in between our drinks," said Bobbi as they debated between mojitos and lemon sours. "

"Yes," Jo agreed, "great idea. Don't want a hangover."

The barman took their order and gave them the water before going off to make the cocktails.

Jo took a sip and pulled a face. "Ergh, water is so boring," she complained. "It makes me feel so waterlogged."

Bobbi laughed loudly. The barman came back with their drinks.

"You want another for your mate?" He hitched a shoulder towards Gail who was now sitting on the bar stool two down, swinging around and grinning like a loon.

"Jesus, imagine her drunk," Jo laughed.

The barman snorted. "She looks proper drunk to me. All

those vodka, lime and bitters are doing their thing."

Bobbi and Jo looked at each other warily. "Were you ordering vodkas?" Bobbi asked Jo.

"Not me."

The barman frowned. "That's what you both asked for, innit?" He looked nervous.

He'd obviously misheard them. Probably the accent and the loud music.

"Shit, she's not an alcoholic, is she?"

Jo gave him a reassuring smile. "I don't think so, no. Don't worry about it, it's all good. It might be best if we don't get her another drink though."

They turned to look at Gail who grinned down the bar at them. "Yoo-hooo," she called loudly. "Let's sing."

"Oh, yes, karaoke," Jo clapped and Bobbi groaned.

Luckily she was saved by the appearance of Jen, looking very flustered and dishevelled, pulling them towards the door. "Hurry up," she screeched, "we have to peg it."

At the door, Raya was ushering Teressa and the other girls out onto the sidewalk.

"Where are we going?" Jo asked.

"And why?" Bobbi added as she downed her cocktail before leaving the glass on the nearest table.

"There was a small incident—" Jen started.

"What the hell?" There was a commotion in the back of the bar and then a bartender shouted out "*We've got a flood!*"

Water was pouring out from the restrooms, soaking into

the carpet.

And then the party were off, running down the street, sashes and feather boas flapping behind them. Bobbi and Jo looked at each other, shrugged, and went with them.

They all ducked into another bar, gasping for breath and laughing.

Jen, it seemed, had decided a shag on the sink was a good idea. The sink, however, did not concur.

"When you think about it, it's not very safe for all the poor disabled people, is it?" Jen complained indignantly. "It's not like I'm that heavy. It should be able to hold up to a bit of a jiggle without coming loose from the wall, you know what I mean? I could totally sue, like."

They were all laughing uproariously and talking about Jen's bad luck, and that it was lucky she and Dave hadn't had an embarrassing sex injury, when Teressa suddenly said, "Shit. Where's Gail?"

They looked around silently and realised they'd left her at the karaoke bar. Cara volunteered to go find her and after she left, Madeline sighed with relief. "I know this will sound awful," she slurred, "but I kinda hope they don't come back."

She looked around them imploringly. "I mean, Cara's lovely, but I feel so guilty whenever I look at her, for stealing her man."

"And now marrying him," added Jen sagely.

Bobbi snorted and Jo frowned at her.

"But Gail," Madeline continued, "I just don't think she

likes me." She looked at her friends. "Why doesn't she like me?" she wailed.

"At least Donny loves you," sniffled Raya. They all looked at her. "He loves you so much he wants to marry you already." She looked ready to cry. "Six bloody years I've been with Steve. Six years and no bloody ring. The bastard."

It would seem they'd reached the teary stage of the evening.

"Shit," Jen said. Then she thumped the table and said, "Fuck this. We need more drinks."

"I'll go," said Leticia.

"I'll help you." Katie got up and trailed after her.

"Oh look, there's an ice bar," cried Teressa. "Come on, girls, harden up."

"We should probably get going," said Jo.

Bobbi nodded.

"Oh please, just one more drink," begged Madeline.

"Well, maybe just one ..." said Jo.

CHAPTER 12

Jo

It was late, or rather early morning, when they stumbled back to the hostel. They'd got a little bit lost, Bobbi insisting she knew the way and ended up walking in the entirely wrong direction. If it hadn't been for the nice couple who had walked with them to make sure they'd got back safely, Jo didn't know where they'd be right now. Neither of them normally had this much stamina for late-night drinking sessions but they felt almost like they hadn't adjusted to the time zone change yet and it still felt like late evening. It was always strange to be on holiday while the rest of the world went on as normal around you. There was a lot you could blame on jet lag and disorientation when you were on the other side of the world.

Bobbi clattered around trying to find the key — there were only two, one for the front door of the hostel and another for the room, but she still couldn't seem to find the right one.

"Fuck's sake, how many bloody keys are there?" she muttered, finally turning the lock.

"Shhhh," Jo admonished in a loud whisper, leaning into the door and stumbling inside, where she hastily threw herself onto the bottom bunk.

Bobbi was apologising profusely to the young lady leaning against the wall for bumping into her. "Aren't you cold in that bikini?" she slurred. There was no reply; the bikini-clad young lady just looked at her steadily. "You look familiar. Have we met somewhere before?"

There had been a rustling sound coming from one of the single beds, with the unseen roommates, but it was silent now.

"You sneaky bitch," Bobbi hissed, when she saw Jo had slithered onto the bottom bunk. She took off her jacket and skirt and with reckless abandon flung them in the general vicinity of her bag before unsteadily climbing the ladder to the top bunk.

Within minutes, Jo could hear her snoring. She shuffled around trying to get comfortable on the hard mattress, worried because she really, really needed to fart and feeling pretty sure whoever else was in the room was now awake.

She tried to lie perfectly still, letting a little bit of gas escape at a time. Her head was spinning and she felt a bit queasy. The last time she'd been this drunk was, well, actually, so long ago she couldn't even remember. Not even at Bobbi's fortieth when Bobbi had closed the bar and had a big party that had gone on until the sun came up. Jo was convinced now that the bunk bed was levitating and it briefly crossed her mind that Bobbi might bump her head on the ceiling and perhaps she should wake her up to warn her.

There was more rustling from the single bed, and then a kind of wet slapping noise and a lot of moaning. What the heck? Was someone having sex?

"Seriously?" she muttered, and put her head under the covers to block the sound. At that moment, she couldn't contain it any more and a massive fart ripped from her. It smelled disgusting; like cauliflower and blue cheese. Jo gagged, sat up and vomited — a stream of cauliflower wings, arancini balls and assorted alcohol — across the floor.

At least this seemed to halt all nocturnal activity from the bed opposite and she fell back onto the mattress and immediately into a drunken slumber.

CHAPTER 13

Bobbi

'For the love of God. Why do they make oven timers so loud?' Bobbi wondered as she tried to reach across to turn it off before her cookies got too crunchy. Bobbi loved them soft and chewy and they were smelling so good.

There was a weird lurching feeling and then she was falling, landing with a thump on the floor of the hostel.

"Fuck."

Her head throbbed, and now her arm did too. There was a disgusting smell that seemed to be coming from the boots next to their bed.

Holy Mother of God. This wasn't good. She suspected she was still rather drunk. Was she going to barf? Jesus. Her mouth felt like the bottom of a rat cage. She was never drinking again.

"Jo," she croaked, "wake up."

There was a muffled groan from the bottom bunk.

"Fuck off."

Bobbi wasn't sure if that was Jo or one of their weird roommates.

"Seriously, Jo, I think I've broken my bloody arm, wake up."

◇

At the A&E they shared a sterile waiting room with a homeless person with a bad cough and even worse odour, a young couple with a grizzling baby, and four young men who had been in a brawl. Bobbi moaned and groaned about the pain, partly in the hope she'd get seen sooner. Jo seemed to be concentrating on her breathing and Bobbi hoped she wouldn't throw up.

She was still wearing the top she'd worn out that night as well as a pair of pink flamingo pyjama pants and her high-heeled shoes, hastily pulled on in the dark. Jo had fortunately fallen into bed fully dressed but smelt like she'd been soaking in a bathtub full of tequila.

They sipped paper cups of water and read the out-of-date gossip in the tattered magazines to pass the time.

Eventually they were seen by a very lovely middle-aged woman doctor, who sent her for X-rays. Bobbi had been a little disappointed, she informed Jo while they waited for the results, that they hadn't gotten a hot young male doctor or nurse to ease her pain.

Still, she was glad she'd taken out travel insurance and felt quite grown up for that. A lot better than the time she'd come off that scooter in Rarotonga in her twenties and had a gross scar on her knee to show from it. Turns out, there were some benefits to getting older and more mature.

More than two hours later they were finally outside, blinking in the early-morning light. Bobbi's arm was bandaged and in a sling.

"Lord, I need a coffee," moaned Jo as she shrugged into her coat and helped Bobbi with hers.

"Or a drink? Hair of the dog," suggested Bobbi.

"You *cannot* be serious?" Jo looked aghast.

"What? It's just a sprain. I'm pretty sure the pills they gave me are only like Panadol and I'm sure you can still drink on them."

"Bobbi," Jo started, her expression pained, "last night you were so drunk, I came back from the loo to find you and Teressa sitting on that ice bar, doing shots out of some poor woman's artificial leg. You can't possibly think we are going to drink again today?"

So that explained the weird ice burns on the back of her thighs. And the thought of shots wasn't so appealing. She suspected they were both still a little bit drunk. Jo smelt rather ripe, now that she thought about it. Perhaps they didn't need more alcohol.

"Coffee it is," she said. "But first, I need to buy a pair of trousers."

◇

Both of them were feeling much better after a hearty breakfast and three Americanos each. There hadn't been any clothing shops open that early so Bobbi decided to brazen it out and act like it was normal to wear your pyjama pants out for breakfast.

"When I lived in West Auckland, no one thought anything of people in the supermarket wearing their dressing gowns and slippers, or even a onesie," she told Jo. "It's not like anyone knows me here anyway. Maybe I'll even start a new trend?"

Jo looked doubtful. But she wisely kept quiet.

"It's probably more embarrassing for *me* to be seen with you looking like that than it is for you," Jo muttered under her breath as a lady walking her dog gave them a wide berth. Bobbi grinned at Jo and made a deranged growling noise at the woman, who lurched into an awkward speed walk, pulling the small dog behind her.

As they walked back to the hostel to meet Adam and grab their bags, they talked about what to wear that night at the concert. It was too cold without a jacket but they both hated having to hold on to them once they warmed up. It was looking decidedly like it might rain again, and Bobbi was glad she'd packed the scarf and beanie that she pulled on as they walked. Doreen would be telling them 'I told you so' for not bringing an umbrella, she thought.

They wandered down the street, trying to get their bearings.

"Oh, maybe you'll see Andre again?" Jo teased.

"Why do all the super-hot men have to be dicks? Anyway,

I'm looking for my Prince Wesley, not Andre the bloody gi-ant," Bobbi grumbled.

"Come on," Jo said gently. "To be fair, he didn't say what he did to hurt you. And he's so hot, you'd have been in for that ride, surely."

Bobbi was silent for a bit.

"You know, it's been a while," she said quietly.

"What's been a while?"

"Since I've been for a ride."

Jo laughed. "What, a few weeks? Come on, Bob, this is *you* we're talking about. You love men."

"Yeah, but I own a predominantly gay drag bar, Jo," she laughed. "It's kinda slim pickings. To be honest, there really hasn't been anyone since Leo."

"Seriously?" Jo looked shocked. "But that was *years* ago, Bob."

"I know, believe me, I know," she shrugged. "I'm actually kind of nervous at the thought of it."

Jo nudged Bobbi's good arm and said, "Well, it's like they say, Bob, when you're a bike ..."

Bobbi laughed and lightly punched her back. "Well, let's see how you feel when you meet some guy and he's keen for a shag. How many guys have you even been with apart from Marcus?"

Jo looked a bit taken aback. "Christ," she muttered, "may-be we do need a drink."

◇

Adam had left a message for them at reception to say he'd gone to the National Football Museum to have a nosy and left his cell number. Jo put it into her phone. They decided to collect all their bags and cab to the slightly better hotel they'd found near the arena.

The plan had been to do a walk around the botanical gardens, but Bobbi decided she needed a nap. Jo was keen to try to get through some more of her book. Perhaps they needed a bit of a down day to recharge.

As they entered their shared room they found their dorm mates in the midst of a heated argument. He was waving a pair of soaking wet boots around, shouting at her in German. She kept shaking her head and gesturing at the top bunk. There was a tangible smell of disinfectant with an underlying whiff of vomit. Awkward. They grabbed their stuff and crept out, Bayley tucked under Jo's arm.

◇

After a quick stop on the way, where Jo jumped out to grab wine and snacks at a liquor store, they checked into the hotel and then showered since they had missed the chance to experience that joy again at the hostel that morning. Bobbi had used one of the bottle shop carry bags on her bandaged arm, thankful that they'd had plastic ones. She had to leave her hair. Way too hard with one arm.

The hotel hadn't even blinked at them showing up with a cardboard cutout and Bobbi in her flamingo pyjama pants, and obligingly had let them check in early. Now Bayley was resting by the window so she could see the view of the red brick wall next door. They both settled on the beds and Jo pulled out her battered paperback. Bobbi lay back and closed her eyes. After about half an hour, Bobbi sat back up. She couldn't get comfortable, and she was sure Jo had been reading the same page for what seemed like an hour.

"What the hell are you reading anyway? That's the same book you had on the plane and you normally read like it's an Olympic sport."

Jo sighed.

"It's called *In Watermelon Sugar*, but I just can't get into it. It's kind of weird."

Bobbi cracked up. "*Watermelon Sugar*? As in a book with the same name as a Harry Styles song? You're crazy, sis." She got up to use the loo. "Shall we go do something? Maybe there's a tour we can do. Chuck me my iPad, will you?"

Jo tossed it over to her.

"Maybe we should get some culture?"

"We may as well," Jo sighed, throwing the book onto the end of her bed. She got up and started to pack their day bag while Bobbi googled tours and attractions. Jo unzipped the side pocket and took something out which she placed on the bedside table. It was a bedazzled cigar box and it looked oddly familiar. The lid was taped shut with a couple of sticking plasters.

Bobbi looked up from the screen and eyed it suspiciously.

"Wait. Is that ... that's the box that was in our room at the B&B in Birmingham."

Jo glanced up. "Oh, yep, I kind of stole it," she replied casually, continuing to pull things out of the backpack and put other things in. "Uncle Bill's box got a little soggy when my water bottle leaked and that awful Jolene isn't going to miss one little trinket from that hideous room. I'm sure it's not valuable or anything."

Bobbi snorted with something like admiration. "You do surprise me sometimes, Josephine."

"There was a little bit of spillage when I transferred him. I just hope I got all the important bits in there," Jo confided.

◇

They were in the shoe section of Selfridges. They'd tried culture, but the tour guide just didn't like them. Probably because Jo kept repeating everything he said as if she were also leading the tour and adding her own little snippets of information. Bobbi had heard him say something quite rude under his breath. She wondered whether Jo was still a little drunk.

He'd asked them to leave. Tried to give them their money back even. Said he was having 'a week' and just couldn't deal with any more crazy women. Bobbi was feeling a bit spacey herself actually and probably shouldn't have offered to give him a cuddle.

So they'd gone to buy a few little gifts and Bobbi had picked up a cute jersey and some earrings for herself. She hoped the top would fit. She couldn't be arsed trying it on and dealing with her arm, so she'd just guesstimated. It was the way she often shopped, as she wasn't a fan of dressing rooms.

They'd have to think about getting something for their parents at some stage too, but didn't want to lug it around with them the whole trip. They'd learnt their lesson when they'd gone round the States and taken too much luggage. Paying extra for overweight bags sucked, so now they tried to pack as light as possible. But it was colder than she'd been expecting and she really needed something warmer. Besides, she could always donate any clothes she got sick of to a homeless person.

Jo had done that once in Vancouver. Bobbi had gone to pick up some dinner for them, and when she got back, Jo had gone through their stuff and gotten rid of shoes, tops and coats. Taken them down the road to some people sleeping rough. Bobbi had not been impressed initially, but the next day when she was still struggling to zip up her bag, she conceded that perhaps her second favourite pair of Converses *had* gone to a better place. She was a much better packer these days.

It was always the shoes that got her though, she mused now as she hobbled across the shoe store to Jo with just one boot on. When she'd realised she couldn't unzip the red latex thigh-high she was trying on with only one hand, it seemed supremely funny. It only got more amusing when Jo pulled and heaved at the offending boot but also struggled to get it off her hoof. Quite frankly, she blamed her mother for her too-big calves. It was obviously genetic. Jo had to straddle Bobbi's leg and was tugging vigorously away on the boot when the inevitable, when it came to Jo, happened. The boot came free, Jo flew backward and landed on her bum. At the same time she let out an enormous fart. It was so loud a lady the next aisle over popped her head up in a panic, staring at them in shocked horror.

Bobbi was lying on the floor, trying to control her bladder, hysterically snorting, tears running down her face, when the stench hit.

"Why the hell does that smell like rotten cauliflower?" she managed to get out before she and Jo were asked to leave by the surly shop assistant.

It wasn't the first time, it wouldn't be the last, thought Bobbi, wiping her eyes as they left the department store to meet up with Adam for an early dinner.

CHAPTER 14

Jo

The pizzas looked great. Jo had ordered two for the three of them to share as well as a bowl of fries. Adam was tucking in with gusto. He had been listening quietly, seeming somewhat amused while she told him about their quest to scatter Uncle Bill's ashes in Scotland, Bobbi interjecting every few seconds.

"Do you always finish each other's—"

"Cocktails?" chorused Jo and Bobbi.

"Yes, we do," laughed Jo. "It's a sister thing, I think. Do you have brothers or sisters?"

"My sister Hannah's at uni in Birmingham. I stayed at hers while I was there."

"So what about you, Adam, are you at school?"

Adam chewed on his thumbnail. "I was at school, I sorta left recently," he mumbled, scooping up a slice of pizza, concentrating on folding it before taking a large bite.

Jo was surprised. "Oh, you seem young to have left school. What are you going to do now then?"

Adam's eyes sparkled as he told them about his plans to be a musician and how he was in a band at school but he'd really like to perform on his own. He'd always loved music.

"My mam was a piano teacher. She taught me and my sister for years, since I was about seven, except Hannah hated it. I taught myself guitar too, and I can play a bit of sax."

Adam was looking down at the table, fiddling with the edge of the checked table cloth and seemed to be deciding whether to speak again or not. "My mam died when I was thirteen. My da couldn't have me and Hannah around so he sent us to school."

He picked up his Coke and slurped it, his eyes fixed on the ice cubes.

"Oh, sweetheart, I'm so sorry to hear that." Jo awkwardly patted his arm.

"That sucks balls," Bobbi added.

"How does your dad feel about you leaving school?" Jo asked.

"I'm gonna tell him soon, I guess."

"So he's okay with you being at these concerts and travelling around on your own? And not having anywhere to stay?"

"Um ... well ..."

Bobbi looked at him sharply. "He doesn't know, does he?"

Adam didn't speak. "He'd be worried sick," Jo finally said,

looking worried sick herself.

Adam shrugged. "Na," he said roughly. "He's so busy with his business, he won't have even been thinking about me." Then added: "He has a whisky distillery. Kinnards. Everyone who makes whisky in Scotland seems to use their surname as their brand." He picked up another slice. "It's kind of lame, I reckon. I'd call it something cool if it was me."

Jo was aware he was trying to change the subject. She let it slide. Poor kid, it sounded like he'd had a bit of a rough time. It can't have been easy losing your mum and then having a dad who was too busy to notice what his kids were going through. Adam seemed like a lovely kid and she'd like to tell the dad to pull his head in.

"So where are you taking your uncle to?"

"A priory on the southeast coast. No idea why, but I do know Uncle Bill was a big fan of Benedictine and they had monks at the priory once, so maybe that's it," Bobbi told him. "We have a letter we have to open when we get there, with instructions."

"No way, not Coldingham?"

"Yeah, that's the one. Do you know it?"

"Sick. That's near my village, St Abbs. Unreal. There's not much out there though."

"Bill was a funny old character. Remember the boot, Bobbi?"

For Adam's benefit she added, "Every Christmas he used to get this ancient boot out and he'd drink a shot from it. So gross. We always thought it was a Scottish thing. Is it?"

Adam had a horrified look on his face. "I've never heard of that tradition but the Scots do have some weird ones."

He sucked the last dregs from his Coke. "I designed the bottles for my da's whisky — they're shaped like a butterfly — and now he thinks I'm going to take over the business one day, but there's no way I'm living out in the boring countryside. He probably thinks music is just a waste of time."

"Well, I don't know your dad, but I'm pretty sure he wants you to be happy," Bobbi said. "Anyway, tell us about the soccer museum?"

"Football," Adam corrected, but the change of subject was a good one, Jo thought, when Adam was still talking about it ten minutes later.

Their waitress came over to see if they wanted desserts or more drinks. They were running out of time, so they declined and asked for the bill.

The cashier wasn't overly cheerful. She hadn't been impressed when they'd shown up with Bayley and Jo had jokingly asked for a table for four. Just insisted they coat-check her, and pay the fee for it too.

But Jo thought she looked tired, and she was following Harry's mantra to 'Treat people with kindness', so she made sure to tip her generously as they left for the concert.

CHAPTER 15

Adam

Adam was pretty sure the cute guy in his line was checking him out. He was tall. Taller than Adam, and fit. His biceps looked nice in his tight T-shirt. Adam wasn't muscular. He played football and he was lean. But he supposed he had an all right arse, and that's what Mr Hottie was looking at. He thought.

He tried smiling at the guy. It felt so awkward. Argh, he had no game.

He probably thought Adam was there with his mum. Or mums. Jo and Bobbi were pretty cool, but he still didn't want the guy to think he was with them because he was too young to be at a concert alone. He inched up a bit to create a gap from them. In any case, they seemed really busy talking to the girls behind them. Jo had a bag of crisps she was sharing around the line.

Should he go up to him? What would he say? And what if people thought he was cutting the line?

Wait, that was definitely him smiling. There was for sure eye contact happening. Oh gawd, he was beckoning him over.

He looked back and saw Jo talking earnestly to a camera crew that were there filming the fandom. The reporter seemed to be going down the line, asking people all sorts of questions about their dedication to Harry. Shit, he definitely did not want to get on the news. If his da saw him, he'd be screwed. He had to move, so he put on what he hoped was a casual yet relaxed smile, and attempted to saunter over to Mr Hottie.

Mr Hottie was called Jack. He was a first-year uni student studying design. Jack had a hip flask and said he and his mates had pre-loaded at the dorms before they came. He offered Adam a drink. He'd paused for a minute before declining. Jack hadn't seemed worried though, which was a relief. Adam wasn't that keen on alcohol. The irony of that was not lost on him but his da reckoned he'd acquire a taste for whisky over time. He had the odd beer, and that was okay, he supposed.

He was 100% sure that Jack was into him. He'd flirted with Adam, touching him on the hand and even slinging an arm around his waist, resting his hand on Adam's hip at one point.

Jack was very chatty and Adam was pretty confident he was going to be his first real snog. He didn't count all the spin-the-bottle kissing with girls in year nine. He wanted his first real, fancy someone and they fancy ya back, pash. Bloody hell. This was shaping up to be one of the best nights of his life. Jack's friends had called out to him so they'd exchanged numbers and arranged to try to meet up either inside or after the show.

Jo and Bobbi had tickets in the mosh pit this time, which was cool 'cause at least he wasn't standing by himself. He'd told Jack the story about Bayley and he'd laughed. He had quite a loud laugh. He and his mates were all quite loud actually. He could see them a bit in front of them shouting and heckling all the people right up the front of the mosh.

They were about ten metres back from the stage and Jo was trying to make sure Bayley was as visible as possible. Her cardboard feet had been resting in something wet, and they were a little mushy, so it was hard to stand her up. Plus someone behind them had punched her head when it blocked his view and now her neck was a little bit bendy. They might have to put some tape on her for the Glasgow show.

Adam couldn't wait to see what Harry wore tonight. He had some incredible suits. Well, he really wore everything well. Adam wished he could wear nail polish at school. He'd do it like Harry's. Maybe he should grow his hair? Do the bandana thing? But he wanted to be his own person too. He wrote his own songs and he thought he was a good singer. People always told him he had talent. He just needed to find his own look, he guessed. He wanted to be a success like Harry, not *be* Harry.

◇

It was nearing the end of the concert, and he was starting to lose his voice from all the singing and screaming. He noticed Jack stumbling through the crowd towards the exit, so he motioned to Jo and Bobbi that he needed some water. Jo said she'd come too, for a bathroom stop. Actually, Adam realised he needed to take a leak too. Bobbi was busy helping some girl fix up her top or something, so they pushed through the crowd without her.

Jo motioned to him she'd get drinks and to wait outside the men's for him. She propped Bayley up against the wall and he gave her an okay signal, then pitched into the bathroom. Jack was there. Adam's heart was suddenly racing.

"Hey, hot stuff," he said and cringed internally. Lame, Adam. Lame. Who the hell said shit like 'hot stuff'? He was such an eejit.

Jack didn't seem to mind, or maybe he hadn't noticed. He grinned and sort of lurched into Adam, putting his palm on his chest and backing him up, out the door and back towards the foyer. He was swaying quite badly and when he slurred "Com'ere", Adam realised he was quite drunk. He could feel his heart beating. This was it, he thought with anticipation, finally, after wondering for so long what his first snog would be like. Only Jack seemed to be having trouble focusing.

"Are you—" he started, only to reel back in horror when Jack proceeded to barf all over him. Like all over him. It dripped down his top, his pants, onto his trainers. The smell was terrible. Adam didn't do well with vomit. Never had. Even someone retching could give him the boak. He tried to hold his breath and not breathe in, but his stomach was clenching and churning. Bloody hell. He did not want to hurl.

Jack had slumped down on his knees on the red paisley carpet. He was groaning and dry heaving. Why were there always chunks of carrot in vomit!?

This was not the best night of his life after all.

◇

Luckily Jo arrived, went into mum mode and took over.

She called over an arena worker to get a medic for Jack, who wouldn't look Adam in the eye. Produced wipes that Adam had used on his neck and hands, and to remove the chunks from his shoes.

She even gave him gum and the minty taste was helping take the smell away somewhat.

She purchased him a Fine Line T-shirt from the merchandise stand. He'd chucked his old one, even though it was one of his favourites. His jacket seemed to be relatively unscathed luckily, and, being leather, had wiped down pretty easily.

He'd tried sponging his jeans off with water and paper towels and they were still rank, but at least they were black and you couldn't tell too much. He still stank though, so he waited outside with Bayley while Jo went in to find Bobbi so they could head back to the hotel and he could have a shower.

Fuck my life, he thought.

CHAPTER 16

Bobbi

Her name was Monique, and her excuse for a top had popped all but one button. Her friends thought it was hilarious but the poor girl was close to tears. Man, Bobbi thought, I'd forgotten what cows girls could be sometimes.

And how had they not frozen their perky little tits off turning up in those clothes in this weather?

"Come here, sweetheart. I'll help you fix it," she shouted over the music.

It took her a while to sort it. Her mind felt a bit fuzzy with drinks and painkillers but eventually she managed to fasten what she thought wasn't too bad of a halter top using her sling. Years of wardrobe malfunctions at the club had paid off.

By the time she'd done the hugs and teary thank yous, she'd managed to lose Jo and Adam.

Still, how hard would a cardboard cutout be to spot?

As it turns out, quite.

Plan B, she decided, was to ask Andre to survey the crowd for her from his distinct vantage point. But it was hot and crowded, and not as easy as she thought it would be to push her way into the hordes towards the stage. People kept jostling her arm, which was starting to throb like a bastard. She tried waving at him with her good arm, and at one point she thought he might have seen her. It was hard to tell on a man with such a stoic face. He stood, arms crossed, scanning the arena intently, seemingly oblivious to the show. Just there to do his job. It made Bobbi want to hassle him, see if she could get a reaction from him, like a guard at Buckingham Palace.

She felt like she was making a little bit of ground, trying to move young girls aside without looking like an arsehole. She could finally see the front of the stage, when there was a surge from behind pushing her forwards.

The high heels may have been a mistake, she had time to think, before she was going down, high-pitched shrieking, feet everywhere and panicking (from them and her). Then suddenly, mercifully, there were arms, scooping her up, high into the air, and there was bloody Andre, rescuing her, like an indomitable, firm-chested knight in shining security T-shirt. "Red," he growled, "I think you may be trouble."

"Inconceivable," spluttered Bobbi and he grinned. And man, that was hot. She became very aware all of a sudden that she was wearing a very short skirt, his hand was holding her bottom, and he smelt like leather and oak. She wanted to hear him laugh, or maybe moan, with his deep gravelly voice and then he had to open his mouth and grunt out the most perfect thing ever: "Babe, I don't think that means what you think it means," and that was that. Bobbi was in love.

"You a'right, babe?" he asked as he set her gently down in the foyer. "Your arm okay?"

"Yeah, yeah, thanks. I appreciate the help. Truly. I'm Bobbi, by the way." Why did her voice sound all breathless when he was the one who'd been carrying her not-insignificant weight?

"Well, Bobbi," he smirked, "I gotta say, the pleasure was all mine," and he winked. Hot. So damn hot.

"Sorry, but I gotta get back, might see you around?"

"I bloody hope so," whispered Bobbi to his retreating back.

◇

The hotel didn't have a bar, which was why they'd picked up the wine to drink in their room. Adam had already gone to his and shut the interconnecting door. They heard his shower start up. He'd been a little quiet on the way home but he seemed okay. Jo had started a singalong at one point and Adam's voice really was beautiful.

Jo lay Bayley down on one of the twin beds and went into the bathroom where she grabbed the plastic, wrapped cups off the sink, then slugged in a hefty amount of wine. She handed Bobbi one.

"Did you know, hotel glasses can be the dirtiest part of the room? In fact, eleven out of fifteen hotels don't clean their glasses at all. So drinking from these is much more hygienic." She raised the plastic cup up in a salute.

"You, Jo, are a wealth of useless information," Bobbi said sardonically, taking the cup in her good hand.

"It's all the random stuff I proofread," Jo sighed. "Sometimes, weird stuff just sticks in there." She tapped the side of her head.

They leaned back against the headboards and sipped their drinks. Wine always tasted slightly odd when it wasn't in a proper wine glass, Bobbi thought to herself. A bit cheaper.

"Poor Adam," said Jo after a bit, "I really feel so bad for him."

"He was all right, it'll wash off," Bobbi replied, downing another pill with the wine. She needed to make another sling for her arm, so she rummaged around in her bag, looking for a scarf that would work.

"Hey, give me one of those, will ya?" Jo pointed at the pill packet. "My head's killing me."

The concert had been just as good as the one in Birmingham but the constant thump of the music and the noise the crowd made was overwhelming.

Bobbi put her cup on the bedside table, threw the pill packet at Jo, and flopped down on her back.

"Seriously, Jo, it's love," she sighed.

"So you've mentioned. Several times," Jo said wryly. "But I agree, it could well be love. Lust at least. He's bloody hot. A bit scary, but hot. You'll have to make a move at the Glasgow show."

Bobbi sat up and retrieved her drink. "Oh yes, what will we wear? Oh, my God, we should totally get kilts."

Jo looked dubious. "Do women even wear kilts?"

Bobbi pondered. "Hmmm, good point, but they're a skirt after all, so why not?"

"Kilts are not sexy. At least, not on a female. Remember as kids when Doreen made us those awful matching, scratchy tartan skirts?"

Jo shot off the bed and grabbed her iPad. It was so sudden Bobbi lurched in surprise and spilt her wine down her top.

"Shit. We'll need to do some washing soon," she grumbled. "What the hell are you doing?"

Jo looked up from the screen.

"Googling bakeries in Glasgow. I just had a thought. I'm sure I read that Harry loves carrot cake. We could get one made and put a Bayley cake topper on it."

"How the hell will we get it to him? I'm *not* staking out his hotel."

Jo thought for a bit. "You could give it to Andre? Two birds, one stone."

Bobbi still wasn't convinced it was the best plan, but it did involve Andre, so she contemplated it. "Sort of like taking Muhammad to the mountain?" She paused. "That is a mountain I'd be keen to climb."

Jo laughed. "Oh, you've got it bad."

Jo drank some more wine while Bobbi managed to pull off her top, take it into the bathroom and run the water into the sink to try to get out the wine stain.

After a bit, Jo called out, "What was Adam's last name, Bob? Was it Killan?"

"No, Kinnain, I think? Or maybe Kinnard? Yeah, I think Kinnard. Why?" She pulled out her pyjama top and wriggled into it.

"Just thinking," said Jo. She picked up her iPad again. Bobbi peered over her shoulder while she googled. Kinnard, whisky, St Abbs. There was a Kelly Kinnard as the first entry. Clan Kinnard Whisky. With a butterfly-shaped bottle sitting on an old wooden bench, a pile of oak barrels behind it. There was a brief history of the distillery. And a contact phone number.

CHAPTER 17

Jo

Jo stared at the web page, tapping her finger on the screen, deep in thought, then pushed her iPad aside. She leaned back against her pillow again and sipped her wine. Bobbi waved the bottle towards her with her good hand and Jo held out her cup for a refill.

"Thanks for doing this, Bob."

"Doing what?" her sister asked, adjusting the bright patterned scarf she was using as a sling.

"Coming with me to see Harry. I know it's a bit of a harebrained idea and there's probably less than a one per cent chance we'll get to meet him, but it's been fun, hasn't it?"

"It *has* been fun. I always have fun with you though. And now I have another new favourite musician. That man has some crazy talent."

Jo sighed. "Sometimes I feel like his performance is so—"

"Intimate?"

"Yes, exactly, intimate. It's like you're witnessing a private moment. I feel almost like I'm intruding." Jo smiled a little drunkenly over at Bobbi. She couldn't think of anyone else she'd rather be doing this with. Having a sister was the best, she thought. She and Bobbi hadn't always been so close; as kids they'd fought a lot, as most siblings do. They had different interests and different friends, Bobbi being two years older. But once Bayley had been born, they'd become really close.

"I'm a much better person when I'm with you, Roberta," she told her sister now, slightly slurred.

"You're feeling very sentimental, Josephine. And no, you're not, you're a great person in yourself."

"What are those painkillers anyway? I feel quite woozy." Jo picked up her iPad again. "I've been thinking about Adam, poor kid. If something happened to him, I'd feel quite responsible."

"What's going to happen to him though? We're here to look out for him."

Adam had protested when Bobbi had insisted on paying for the hotel and for the meals but they'd got the feeling he was a bit skint. He'd seemed worried even paying for the hostel the first night and he must have spent a fair bit on his concert tickets. He'd earnestly told her he'd pay her back when he could and Bobbi had agreed, but Jo knew there was no way she'd accept any money from him. Bobbi's big heart was one of the things Jo loved most about her.

"I know, but we can't force him to stick with us, can we? I just keep thinking that I'd want to know if it was Bayley."

"True. You should send his dad a message."

"It's Saturday though. He might not get it until Monday," Jo replied. Decisively she picked up her phone. "I'm just going to call him."

Before she could change her mind, Jo tapped the number on the web page into her phone. It rang a few times and for a moment she had second thoughts. Before she could hang up, the phone clicked and a sleepy male voice answered.

"Hello?"

"Is that ... is that Kelly Kinnard? From the whisky place? Father of Adam and, um, Hannah?"

There was a distinct pause on the other end. "Aye. Who's this?"

"Sorry to call you so late, you don't know me, my name is Jo and we have your son."

"You what? Is this some kind of joke?"

"No, no, sorry. We don't *have* your son. He's with us, I mean. Travelling with my sister Bobbi and me. We're here from New Zealand to see Harry Styles. For my daughter. We haven't taken him hostage or anything sinister like that." Jo knew she was rambling, but couldn't seem to stop.

"My son is in school." Kelly emphasised each word, as though Jo might be slightly mentally impaired.

"But he's not. He's left school. He's been travelling, alone.

And he seems to be ill-prepared for that, I have to say." She hoped she didn't sound too snippy but thought from the look Bobbi gave her that maybe she did.

"He's what? What are you blathering about?"

"Of course, you didn't know this," she added hastily. "I'm sure you're a busy man, but if it were my daughter, I'd definitely want to know."

"Hang on a wee minute. Adam's not in school? That can't be right. The school hasn't rung me." Kelly sounded confused, probably still half asleep.

"I think he may have spun them a story." Jo covered the phone with her hand and turned to Bobbi. "Good Lord, he has a sexy accent."

Bobbi snorted. "I don't think covering the phone works with an iPhone, Jo, you need to mute."

Jo felt herself turning red.

"I beg your pardon?" an alarmed voice was saying on the other end of the line. "Adam is a seventeen-year-old lad."

"Oh no," Jo interjected quickly, "I wasn't meaning Adam had a sexy voice, I ... er ..."

Bobbi had buried her face in the pillow but Jo could see her shoulders shaking with laughter.

"Where are you right now?" Kelly demanded. He didn't sound at all sleepy now.

"We're in Manchester, in a hotel. Separate rooms, of course. Well, Adam has a separate room to Bobbi and me. We're going to catch a train tomorrow to Glasgow—"

"What time will that be? I'll meet you at the station."

Jo and Kelly swapped mobile numbers and she agreed to text him when they knew what time they were arriving.

"Jaysus. What a mess," he said tiredly. Jo was sure she could hear him pacing up and down.

"It's not so bad, I'm sure everything will be fine. He really is a lovely kid," she told him, hopefully in a soothing kind of manner. "I ken how you feel though."

"Aye, you do, do ya?" Kelly replied, sounding a little less grumpy. "Well, if you'll let me know when you arrive, I'd be most grateful and I'll be there to meet you off the train."

They hung up after that. Bobbi was cackling loudly, almost rolling off the bed. "You *ken* how he feels?"

Jo clamped her hands over her face and groaned. "I know! Did I really just say that? I was all overcome by his accent. Too much *Outlander*. Argh, we need more wine."

"You definitely don't need more wine."

But she topped up their plastic cups again anyway.

CHAPTER 18

Bayley

Bayley lay on her bed and adjusted the strap of her slip to sit lower on her shoulder. She ruffled her hair again to make sure it was a little messy. When her phone said 1.30am she put it down on the side table and stood up, taking a calming breath. Then she let out a loud, nervous squeal, opening her door and running down the hall to Bobbi's spare room where she knocked quickly and let herself in.

Sam was only half awake, sitting up in the bed, rubbing his face. "Bayley?" he said in a low, sleepy voice. "Are you okay?"

Bayley did a little theatrical shake and made her voice tremble. "Sam," she said breathily, "I think there's a mouse in my room. I can hear it scratching and I can't sleep in there."

Sam looked at her, his lip twitching slightly before he asked, "Do you want to swap beds?"

Bayley pretended to consider this for a minute. "Well,

maybe," she replied uncertainly. "But if you don't want to move, I guess I could just sleep in here with you? You wouldn't even know I was here."

Sam looked her slowly up and down and Bayley felt a hot rush go through her. She tried to look a little sweet, but not too innocent. It was tricky to get the balance right, she thought.

She'd been working hard on catching his attention the last few days. She wanted him to know she wanted him. But he didn't seem to be getting her subtle hints.

She knew he fancied her. Had seen him looking when she 'accidentally' came out of the shower in a towel as he was walking past. Or when she brushed against him in the bar or they rubbed thighs as they sat side by side on the couch. He was into her, she knew he was. But she suspected he had reservations. That he thought he was too old for her. Or rather that she was too young.

Except he was starting to see her as an equal now as they worked and lived together. Especially now, as she stood at the foot of his bed, in her sexy nightwear that emphasised her legs and cleavage.

Eventually, after what seemed like an unspoken argument with himself, he reached across and pulled the duvet open on the other side of the bed.

Bayley slipped in with a whispered thanks, keeping a modest distance between them.

"Oh, it's cold," she said, after a bit, sliding closer. "Warm me up a bit, will you?"

Sam gave a strangled laugh. "I don't know if that's such a good idea," he croaked, but he had turned towards her. Did he look conflicted? In the moonlight coming in through a crack in the curtains, his eyes rested on her lips and his breathing was uneven.

"Sure it is," Bayley whispered, moving closer again.

His hand came up and he rubbed his thumb along her bottom lip. Her heart thumped painfully.

"Shit, Bayley," he groaned. "Do you know what you do to me?"

Bayley snuggled in closer until their hips were aligned. "I think I have a pretty good idea," she murmured, pressing up against him.

Sam groaned again. "Fuck, Bay," he started, and then she kissed him.

◇

Later, in a tangle of limbs, as she caught her breath, Bayley had said; "You know Aunt Bobbi thinks you're gay, right? Mum too, I think."

Sam laughed. "Yeah, I kinda got that impression," he said with a shrug.

"I can't wait to correct them," Bayley said. They both laughed. Then Sam leant over to kiss her again.

"Perhaps we'd better just make sure," he said, moving down lower. "Oh and Bayley?"

Bayley was smiling dreamily and mentally giving herself a thumbs up.

"Hmmm?" she said distractedly, pushing him lower still.

"I know you're not scared of mice, babe," Sam said, laughing against her belly.

CHAPTER 19

Adam

Adam was fair pissed.

He'd thought Jo and Bobbi were cool, but now they'd talked to his da and everything was going to shite.

He slumped down next to Bayley on the seat. The back of her head had two large sticking plasters holding it up. He focused on them.

Jo tried again to talk to him. "Adam, I'm sorry, I was just—"

Sod it. He didn't have to sit on the train with them. She wasn't his mam. He stood, still not making eye contact, putting in his earbuds as he moved down the aisle and into the next carriage.

He only had a few hours before his da killed him, so he wasn't going to waste time cutting about with traitors.

The morning had started okay. Bobbi had been up early

and washed some of his clothes for him, which was awesome, 'cause he didn't have a lot with him. He had a great sleep in, with the whole queen bed to himself. He was used to the narrow, thin mattress from school, so it was awesome to spread out on the queen. He had his own bathroom so he'd had a long, hot shower without someone yelling at him to hurry up.

They'd had breakfast and all talked about last night's show. The performance had been wicked. Right from the intro. The two of them seemed to have become something of Harry experts, Adam thought. Jo knew a lot of Harry trivia. It was kinda funny. Not that he could talk.

He'd even gotten a text from Jack to say sorry. He'd just sent back a thumbs up. Neither Jo nor Bobbi had asked him anything, but he was pretty sure they'd figured out he was gay. Jo had said it was a shame things hadn't worked out and Bobbi had agreed, but said there were plenty more fish in the sea. They hadn't seemed at all bothered by his sexuality. Not that they should be, but it was a good feeling. They were a similar age to his da, he thought, so it made him feel like maybe his reaction would be okay too.

Bobbi had insisted he get a cooked breakfast and it was magic. Sausage, beans, eggs, the works. Jo had been pretty quiet till after her second coffee, and then she had started asking weird questions like what did his da look like? Was he into any sports? Did he wear a kilt? And Bobbi kept saying 'if you ken what she means' and cracking up until Jo had thumped her.

But then she'd confessed about ringing and talking to his da last night and telling him all about him ditching school. And now Hannah and his da kept texting and trying to call him. And they were both mad as hell, he'd be willing to bet.

He should have just bailed on the Kiwis after breakfast, hung about till the London show. But Glasgow was the one he was most looking forward to. He'd seen 1D there with his mam, back in middle school, before the car accident. Fuck, he missed his mam. They'd been close when he was a kid. They both loved music. That was why he wanted to be a musician. She'd been there for him all the time too. When she died it was so unexpected and he'd often forget she was gone for a few seconds when he woke up. In some ways he was glad when his da suggested boarding school. It was hard to be in the house at first with all her stuff and she wasn't there. But sometimes he just wanted to be back home with the nice memories. He and Hannah didn't really talk much about it. Well, they talked about mam and about stuff they remembered from when she was alive, but they never talked about, you know, 'feelings'. It was kind of something none of them had ever been good at in their family. It was a bit lame, he guessed, but when he sang, or played, especially the piano, he kind of felt like his mam was still listening. Adam would have been able to talk to her about liking boys too. Everything would have been easier if his mam was alive.

He sniffed, wiping his nose with his sleeve and looked up

at the ceiling, blinking rapidly. He'd look like a right tool if he started to cry now. In all honesty, he wasn't sure if he was mad, upset, or scared. All of the above, he supposed.

Adam sent a text to Hannah saying he was sorry he hadn't told her everything and promised to tell their da she didn't know what he was up to, so she wouldn't get into trouble.

His phone rang again, but he didn't want to have a conversation right now and he hit decline before turning up his music and closing his eyes, leaning back against the headrest and trying not to think.

CHAPTER 20

Jo

Fortunately they managed to nab a table seat and Jo placed Bayley by the window again. It seemed to be the best place to stop her sliding all over the train. Poor Bayley wasn't looking her best and was a bit slumped and saggy, as though she were getting tired of chasing after Harry, Jo thought. She sent a quick text off to Kelly Kinnard to let him know which train they were on so he could meet them when they arrived.

Adam had gone off in a huff somewhere, but she was glad they had a seat for him if he decided to come back. She couldn't say she blamed him really. Bayley would have been mad at that age if someone had dobbed her in like Jo had done to Adam. Although she felt bad, she was still convinced she'd done the right thing.

"I got us some water. Maybe I should have grabbed a coffee as well." Bobbi handed Jo a bottle. She was always organised like that. "It would probably be crap though and we'd only be disappointed."

"Yeah, and then we'd be hanging out for a decent coffee for the entire journey. Hopefully there'll be a decent cafe when we change trains."

Jo took the bottle, along with the packet of honey-roasted peanuts Bobbi had bought her. Of course now that Bobbi had mentioned coffee, she was hanging out for one.

Two teenage girls entered the carriage. One of them gave Bayley a measured look, then cracked her gum at Jo and sneered. She pouted and pointed out Bayley's seat number to her friend, who just shrugged.

"Ugly bikini," said the girl. She was wearing a knock-off T-shirt with 'GUCHI' across the front.

"That really rips my undies," Jo whispered to Bobbi, inclining her head towards the misspelled T-shirt as the girl shoved her bag into the overhead luggage rack as they took the seats in front.

"That's probably because of your job. But you've always been anal about spelling and grammar."

"That's not a bad thing," Jo retorted, and Bobbi gave her a grin.

"I never said it was."

The train started to pull out of the station and Jo glanced at Bayley again. She thought briefly of taking a photo and sending it to the real Bayley, who would no doubt find it hilarious that she was on the trip with them, but she probably

should have done that when she was all fresh and new looking. It was a bit late now.

"Bob, I don't think this is working," she said.

Bobbi peered up at Jo over her glasses. She was flicking
through a magazine, but now closed it with a sigh and tossed
it aside.

"What a load of crap, I don't know why I waste my money
on these things. Why do they always claim Jen is pregnant?
I mean that's got to be the longest pregnancy in history,
right? Anyway, what's not working, Josie?"

"Waving Bayley around hoping to get Harry's attention. Two
shows and he hasn't noticed her. Who would have thought a
life-size cardboard cutout would be so easy to miss?"

"Well, I don't know what else we can do. Maybe write on
her head 'Hi, Harry, I'm the future Mrs Styles'?"

There was a loud snort from in front of them. Miss Guchi,
who was apparently eavesdropping, didn't seem to think
that was a very good idea.

Jo thought for a bit. "Maybe we need a catchy sign."

"'Marry me, Harry'?" Bobbi suggested.

"Nah, probably been done before. Just once or twice."

Bobbi laughed. "True. How about 'Marry my daughter'?"

"Oooh, yeah, that's good. Cute."

Jo thought she heard Miss Guchi say "As if," and then,
"Cardboard dummy."

Bobbi must have heard her too because she gave Jo a
questioning look and Jo shrugged. She had no idea what the

girl's problem was.

"We could have a whole heap of signs. I could hold up 'It's a sign'."

Bobbi chuckled. "And I'll hold up 'of the times'." They both laughed loudly.

"What about 'My arms hurt'?" Jo suggested.

Bobbi cackled and offered "The people behind me can't see."

"If you can't read this you're not close enough."

"If you *can* read this you're still not close enough."

Jo snorted water up her nose.

"Dumb," Miss Guchi retorted. She turned and glared at them. "What about 'My daughter's an ugly cow'?" Then she turned back and pulled her woollen hat down over her ears and slumped down into her seat, hopefully no longer listening in to their conversation.

They were stunned into silence for a few seconds, Jo gaping like a fish.

Then Bobbi looked wistful. "I'd really like a sign that said 'Take off your shirt'."

"Bobbi!" Jo slapped her lightly on the hand, as if admonishing a naughty child. "I'm sure that's been done too and he hasn't taken it off yet," she added, somewhat sadly.

"That is unfortunately true, but maybe Andre would see it." Bobbi smiled happily at the thought.

Jo closed her eyes for a few seconds. "What do you think will happen with Adam? I feel bad for him, really, but what else could I have done?"

"I would have done the same thing."

"You would have?" Jo had thought Bobbi would have come up with a much 'cooler' solution. She'd never had to do the day-to-day discipline and had always spoilt Bayley rotten whenever she'd gone to stay with her. It was easy enough being the fun aunty, less so being mum 24/7.

"Of course," Bobbi reassured her. "I'm sure Adam will realise it too, eventually. Remember when you wouldn't let Bay get her nose pierced when she was thirteen? Then when she was fourteen she declared that nose piercings were gross."

Bobbi was grappling with her water bottle, gripping it between her legs and trying to open it with the other hand. She had fashioned a bright-pink tasselled scarf as a sling and it looked very jaunty. "Here, open my water bottle for me, will you? I can't bloody do it one-handed."

"That's what he said," Jo replied with a grin.

CHAPTER 21

Bobbi

"Where do you think Andre is from?" Without giving Jo time to reply, Bobbi added, "I can't believe he quoted *The Princess Bride*. *And* he asked about my sore arm, which was very sweet. And observant." She sighed dramatically. "Could he be any more perfect?"

"It would seem not," Jo replied, rolling her eyes. But she was smiling fondly at Bobbi, and Bobbi grinned back. It was lovely to feel those new, lustful feelings for someone. To have them merging into a perfect person in your imagination, before reality hit. Rose-coloured glasses were awesome. Especially for a holiday fling to get you back on the bike, so to speak.

"Imagine all those men in Scotland for you to lust after, Josie. If you thought Kelly sounded sexy, you'll be in heaven in a few hours, any time a man opens his mouth within a two-metre radius."

Jo looked over her shoulder, presumably to check Adam was still out of earshot and whispered, "He really did sound like he could just *talk* you into a Big O, you know. I wish there'd been a photo of him on the website though. Still, if he looks anything like Adam, he's no ogre." She paused. "I'm quite looking forward to Scotland now actually."

Bobbi agreed. "I wonder if we'll get a chance to try this Kinnard whisky," she pondered.

"Did you know, Jack Daniel learnt how to make whisky from a Lutheran minister when he was only six?' Jo informed her.

"I did not," Bobbi replied.

"And," Jo continued, "whisky is one of the base ingredients for Tabasco sauce. Also, a diabetic's urine can be made into whisky because of the high sugar content."

"Yum," was Bobbi's sarcastic reply.

"Oh, speaking of alcohol, we have to remember to pick up the Benedictine to toast Uncle Bill when we get to this priory he's so keen to be scattered over."

"Christ," grimaced Bobbi, "last time I drank that stuff, I ended up flying down State Highway One in a convertible, with no top on."

Jo gave a shake of her head, as though trying to dislodge an image that was stuck there. "No top on the convertible, or you? Actually, forget that, I don't want to know."

The train to Glasgow was pretty packed, and there were a lot of fed-up-looking passengers. One elderly woman was complaining loudly about the cold coffee and her friend was bemoaning the fact that the toilet on their carriage wasn't working. Bobbi couldn't see a charging plug anywhere, and her phone was nearly flat.

Still, it was nice to sit and not stress about work, or think about boring, daily life. And the scenery was pleasant enough. Trains were one of their favourite ways to get about, especially since Bobbi wasn't the best driver. She didn't use her little Mini much in Wellington and tended to walk most places, so when they were overseas and needed a car, she always made Jo drive. Especially if it was on the other side of the road. Bobbi was the 'navigator', which usually meant she got them somewhat lost, so trains were always their go-to way to get around.

"I might go and see if I can cheer Adam up," Bobbi declared, standing and narrowly avoiding the leg the surly little cow in the Guchi shirt had suddenly stretched into the aisle. Bobbi shot her the finger as she left.

◇

Adam was pretending to sleep. But Bobbi was pretty sure she'd seen him quickly shut his eyes when he saw her coming, so she plonked herself down next to him, placing the can of Coke and the packet of chips she'd got him in his lap. His hand moved to hold on to them, but he didn't look at her.

"Buddy," she started. "Jo's a mum, a nurturer. A caregiver through and through. She was only worried about you." She waited. Adam stayed silent. "You know, your dad had to get wind of this eventually, right?"

She gave his shoulder a small nudge. "You can't just leave school and have no one notice, you know. Believe me, I tried."

Adam cracked open one eye and looked at her.

"Yep. Long, boring story, when I wanted to join a gypsy fair, but Mum and Dad made me go back. And I'm glad I did. School's not so bad really. Which is something no one figures out until they leave. Even Harry says 'stay in school' and he seems like a pretty on-to-it guy, don'cha think?" That earned her a small smile.

Adam opened the Coke and raised the can and his eyebrows in thanks. "I'm sorry if I was a bit of a gobshite, Bobbi. I guess I'm just freakin' about what my da will do when he sees me." He took a big gulp of the drink and then burped softly. "I know I've fucked up, and I'm pretty sure he's gonna go mental."

"Well, maybe. All I can say to that is, no point worrying till ya have to, mate. It might sound trite, but it's true." She pinched a chip as Adam opened up the foil packet. "The worst hasn't happened yet, and maybe it won't. You know, parents really do just want their kids to be happy. Even if it feels like they're ruining or controlling your life sometimes. Talk to your dad. Tell him how you feel." She grinned at him. "*After* he's gone off at you."

Adam gave a small, strained laugh.

"Thanks, Bobbi. Really. You guys have been awesome to

me. Honest."

"Come on," pleaded Bobbi. "Come back and have a singa-long with us. You're the only one of us who can hold a tune."

"Aye, that's true." Adam sniggered. They had just stood up to head back to their carriage when they heard Jo screaming.

CHAPTER 22

Jo

"Bayley!"

Jo had just come back from the bathroom. She rushed over to look out the window, the one the girl had just thrown Bayley out of. There was no sign of her now, she had probably fluttered off into the countryside.

The girl in the Guchi top looked smug, a smirk playing around her mouth and a slightly manic sense of victory in her eyes. It made Jo, uncharacteristically, want to slap her.

"What the hell? Why did you do that?"

"She's not even real," the girl taunted. "Harry's not going to marry a stupid fake cardboard wannabe."

Jo felt strangely upset about losing her cardboard daughter. It had been an experience, she and Bobbi lugging Bayley halfway across the world and around the country and somehow, she realised, it had made her feel as though Bayley had been there along with them for the ride.

At that moment Bobbi appeared, half running, half lurching up the aisle with Adam right behind her.

"Jo? What's going on?"

"This ... young lady ... just threw Bayley off the train while I was having a wee!" Jo yelled.

There was alarmed murmuring from the seats around them. Everyone nearby had focused their attention on Jo and the young girl.

"Let's all calm down. What exactly happened?" A middle-aged man wearing a tweed jacket and serious expression had stood, clearly hoping to sort everything out.

"This girl here has thrown my daughter off the train." Jo glared at the girl, who was looking very sulky now.

There was a collective startled gasp around them. "Stop the train! Someone stop the friggin' train!" someone called.

Somebody else thumped the emergency stop button.

"She was just cardboard," Miss Guchi shouted. "What's the big deal?"

Jo was horrified as she took stock of the situation. She realised she may have overreacted a little and caused a chain of events where everyone around her had also overreacted. There was an ear-splitting, shrieking sound of metal on metal as the train braked. Adam lurched into Bobbi who in turn lurched into Mr Tweed Jacket.

The girl burst into noisy tears and stamped her foot.

"It's not fair," she sobbed. "First that cardboard girl is sitting in seat 1D and then I hear them talking about how she's going to meet Harry Styles."

She sniffed and wiped her nose on the back of her arm.

"So let me get this clear," Tweed was asking slowly. "This wasn't an actual person?"

"Of course it wasn't an actual bloody person," Jo snapped at him. "Do you think this little slip of a thing would be able to haul an adult woman out that tiny window?"

"I had to fold her a bit," Miss Guchi conceded. "But she was quite bendy already."

There was more confused murmuring as everyone tried to piece everything together.

At that moment the conductor arrived, looking very sombre, but also slightly self-important.

"Who pushed the emergency button?"

"A girl went off the train," someone called to him, a person in the back of the carriage who hadn't fully caught up on the details yet. Someone was sobbing loudly.

The conductor started talking into his walkie-talkie.

"No, no, it's not as it seems," Jo said hastily and then went into a rather convoluted explanation of what had transpired. While she did this Bobbi tried to calm the hysteria in the carriage and eventually everyone settled down. Adam had slunk into Bayley's vacated seat, the one numbered 1D that had caused the drama in the first place. Then, having second thoughts about this and eyeing Miss Guchi warily, he changed his mind and quickly slid over to the seat next to it instead.

Jo managed to talk the conductor out of charging Miss Guchi with throwing an object from the train. She also offered to take the rap for the person who panicked and pressed the emergency button. She was then taken to the guard's room where a report was filed. Thankfully, no charges were laid in the end.

He did slip a card into her hand for a counselling service and suggested that, while he had seen stranger things than a passenger travelling with a life-sized cardboard cutout of their daughter, it possibly wouldn't go amiss to talk to someone about it.

Jo returned to Bobbi, who looked relieved to see her. Slumping down in her seat, she ignored all the accusing glares and muttering around her about the delay to their journey. Perhaps it was a good thing they'd be changing trains soon.

CHAPTER 23

Adam

Adam wasn't complaining. They had missed their connecting train and had to wait for another, but the longer that took, the better, to his mind. Any delay suited him if it meant putting off seeing his da.

Jo had asked him to text and let him know they were going to be late, but he was out of data and both Jo and Bobbi's phones were flat.

They'd gone inside at the station to get out of the cold wind, and now they were having hot drinks and sharing a bag of Maltesers. He kept looking around though, feeling like someone was missing. Poor Bayley. He'd miss her.

He and Jo had vaguely made up by not talking about it at all, and instead were having a did-you-know trivia standoff on One Direction facts. Bobbi was alternating over-the-top yawning and sighing with begging them to stop.

He'd decided he would ask his da to give Bobbi and Jo a lift to St Abbs. That way he'd have to wait till they got home to yell at him. Maybe he could even suggest they stay with them. They had a spare room, after all. If he asked in front of them, his da would look rude saying no. That would take the heat off him a bit and he'd have a few days to work on getting to Harry's Glasgow concert.

Anyway, it was a plan of sorts. He ate another Malteser and grinned at Jo when Bobbi stormed off to the loo in a huff.

CHAPTER 24

Bobbi

Luckily, Kelly was still waiting for them when they finally disembarked at Glasgow. They were well over an hour late, and he looked a little stressed.

Bobbi could see the family resemblance as she looked between him and Adam, a glimpse of what Adam would look like in thirty years' time. Kelly wasn't tall, but he was quite stocky and had a rugged, masculine air about him. He was unshaven, with a few days' growth of stubble. His eyes were a lovely hazel and he had a nice, open smile.

He hugged Adam, who seemed surprised, and stood there awkwardly for a few seconds before hugging him back.

"Sorry, Da," he whispered, and Kelly said, "We'll talk soon, lad," before reaching out a hand towards Jo. "Hello, I'm Kelly."

There was a weird pause until Bobbi gave Jo a nudge, causing her to emit a little squeak before she lurched forward to shake his hand. She didn't say anything, so Bobbi had to be the one to say "Hi, Kelly, that's Jo, I'm Bobbi. It's nice to meet you." She shook his hand too and they smiled at each other.

"Thank you so much for accompanying Adam home. I'm truly in your debt."

Bobbi started to say how it was no trouble, and that Adam had been great, but Adam had started speaking quickly over the top of her, fiddling with the cord of his hoodie.

"Actually, Da, I was wondering, seeing as they're headed our way, could we give them a ride back to St Abbs? They need to get to Coldingham Priory."

"Well, aye, of course," Kelly said, sounding sincere, but also shooting Adam a look that Bobbi took to mean that he was on to his plan to delay their discussion. Adam avoided his eye, instead looking about as though everything around him was of huge interest.

"Only if that's not too much of a bother?" Bobbi asked. He shook his head. "Nae, not at all," he insisted.

He took hold of Jo's suitcase beside her, and nodded at Adam to help Bobbi with hers, before pointing towards a white SUV parked nearby. 'Clan Kinnard Whisky' was sign-written on the side.

As they walked, Bobbi apologised for making him wait so long.

"Ahh, dinnae fash yourself," he replied, "'twas no bother. Though did I hear right, there was a body on the tracks?"

"Aye, that was Bayley," Adam told him mournfully. "She was pushed out the window."

Kelly looked up sharply, a concerned look crossing his features. "Who's Bayley?"

Jo chose that moment to finally speak, "Oh, Bayley is my daughter." She smiled at Kelly. He did not smile back. Instead, he stopped dead in his tracks, dropping her suitcase on the kerb with a clatter. "Jaysus, Mary and Joseph," he exclaimed. His face looked horrified.

Adam let out a loud laugh and Jo's face fell as she realised she hadn't mentioned that Bayley had been made of cardboard.

◇

Half an hour into the journey, Adam hadn't said a word and was staring resolutely out the window. Jo was still apologising for the misunderstanding with Bayley, and Bobbi decided it was getting a bit uncomfortable. To lighten the mood, she leaned into the front seat, between Adam and Kelly, and sweetly told Kelly that she thought his accent was very charming. He blushed. Adam looked at him sideways with an unimpressed look. Jo elbowed Bobbi discreetly in the ribs. Hard. "Don't you think, Jo? Quite sexy, isn't it?" It was hard to tell who looked the most uncomfortable, Jo or Kelly, Bobbi mused.

There was a short silence and then Kelly cleared his throat and murmured his thanks before asking them what they were headed to Coldingham for. Between them, they told him about Uncle Bill and his final wishes.

"Is it far from St Abbs to the priory?" Jo asked. "We were hoping we could walk."

"About a half-hour walk I'd say," Kelly replied, "but only a wee drive. Five minutes or so, depending where you're staying."

"Actually, Da, I was thinking they could stay with us," Adam interjected quickly. "We have room, and they haven't booked anywhere yet, right, guys?"

He craned his head round to look at them in the back seat.

Jo looked mortified. "Oh, no, we couldn't possibly impose like that," she exclaimed. "We'll be quite happy at the local hotel or bed and breakfast."

"Absolutely," Bobbi agreed. "Anything will be fine."

Kelly looked across at Adam, who was again pointedly staring out the window, then back at Jo in his rear-view mirror, before saying, "Nae, Adam's right, we have plenty of room, and it wouldn't be a bother at all. Please, do stay with us. I insist." He seemed very sincere, and it seemed rude to argue, so they agreed with thanks.

Adam looked rather pleased with himself, and Bobbi suspected they'd all been quite well played.

CHAPTER 25

Jo

They had a good chance to see the Scottish countryside on the journey and arrived at St Abbs in the early evening.

They made small talk on the way, discussing Uncle Bill and their parents, and where they were from in New Zealand. Kelly told them he'd love to visit New Zealand one day and they told him he was more than welcome to visit them if he ever did. They briefly touched on Jo's separation and Kelly being a widower. And about Bayley and the bar.

Kelly had dropped Adam into the village to buy some fresh seafood for dinner and he'd just returned. Jo and Bobbi could hear a rather heated discussion going on between him and his father while they discreetly stayed in their room, getting settled.

The village was smaller than Jo had expected, but rather pretty with its old stone cottages and white-washed houses crammed onto narrow streets. The sea had been grey but calm, blending into the grey sky above, fishing boats bobbing gently, moored in the harbour.

Kelly's house was quite charming too, rather like its owner, Jo thought. He'd made them feel very welcome, and they were in a lovely guest room. She'd love to add a few feminine touches, she'd told Bobbi, but then Kelly had knocked on the door a few minutes later with a cracked antique jug, full of daffodils he'd just picked from the garden.

When they emerged from their room, Adam was nowhere to be seen, most likely sulking in his room, Jo thought, thinking back to how Bayley had been as a teenager after they'd had an argument. Kelly was cooking in the kitchen, an apron tied around his waist. He had poured two glasses of wine and now handed one to each of them.

"I'm sorry, I didnae ask, but I hope you like red."

"Thanks, yes, we do. I just feel bad we've turned up empty-handed," Jo replied as she took the glass from him and took a sip.

"Ach, that's not a problem. Maybe while you're here we could see if we can find some New Zealand wine to pick up. You must stay for a few days at least and have a look around."

"We don't want to be any trouble," Jo replied, somewhat weakly, thinking it would be quite nice to have a few days relaxing around this little village.

"Nae trouble at all. We don't often get to entertain visitors and it'll stop Adam and me from murdering each other while we sort things out. Now if you'll excuse me, ladies, make yourselves cosy and I'll get back to the kitchen. There's a wee bit of cheese and some crackers on the table in the living room for you."

Adam joined them after a while, as the smell of garlic and onion and seafood wafted temptingly through the house. It seemed to Jo that he and Kelly hadn't fully resolved things yet and he sat and fiddled with his phone, not saying much to anyone. Kelly made an enormous dish of paella, full of fresh fish, prawns and mussels. There was a green salad, a mountain of crusty bread, plus more wine. Adam seemed to come out of his mood a little when his father offered him a beer and he told them a funny story about the time he and Hannah had stolen two beers when Kelly had been at work a few years back. They were worried they'd be in trouble for being drunk. They weren't even remotely, of course, Adam said, laughing, and Kelly hadn't even noticed the beers were missing.

"Let us do the dishes, Kelly," Jo offered as Adam cleared the table.

"Ach, dinnae fash yerself with that."

Adam looked at Kelly and started laughing.

"Da, why are you suddenly sounding more Scottish than usual?"

Kelly gave him a look, turning slightly red. "You're off your head, lad, and for that, you can do the dishes, you cheeky wee clipe."

They settled back into the living room with their wine,

while Adam, grumbling only slightly, took the remaining dishes into the kitchen.

Kelly began to tell them about Clan Kinnard, a business he had taken over from his father when he had retired. Jo was asking him a question about the whisky-making process when Bobbi, who had been uncharacteristically quiet, fidgeting and looking uncomfortable, stood up suddenly.

"Sorry, I'm not feeling too good. If you don't mind, I think I might head off to bed."

"Is everything all right?" Kelly asked.

Bobbi's face had become red and puffy and her eyes were watering.

"I'll be fine, there must be something in the air that's irritating me."

Kelly looked concerned. "You're not allergic to the seafood, I hope? I'm sorry, I didnae even think to ask you."

"No, no, I love seafood." Bobbi paused, brow wrinkled in thought. "There wasn't saffron in the paella, was there?"

"Aye, there was," Kelly replied. "You wouldnae be allergic to that?"

"Yeah, I am. Sorry, I don't usually think to mention it. Not many people use it at home. The paella was spectacular though."

Kelly looked completely alarmed but Bobbi waved him off. "Don't worry about it, it's not life-threatening or anything like that, I'm sure I've got some antihistamines. I'll be fine by the morning."

She left and after Jo had reassured him that Bobbi wasn't going to stop breathing and drop dead, they settled back with their drinks and resumed their conversation.

Adam had finished the dishes by now and rejoined them with another beer.

Jo told them about an ex of Bobbi's who had taken a large quantity of a saffron supplement, as it worked as a natural Viagra. Bobbi had looked a lot worse that time, she laughed.

"The problem was that it wasn't just internally he'd taken the saffron, if you get what I mean."

Kelly roared with laughter and Adam looked confused, then blushed bright red when Jo explained: "He'd applied it to another part of his body."

Adam's horrified reaction made Kelly and Jo laugh even harder. Jo sloshed wine on the leather armchair and then wiped it up with the sleeve of her cardigan.

"Is that why you use it in *your* cooking, Da?" Adam joked once they calmed down, and Kelly retorted, "Rest assured, lad, I've nae need of that."

Adam left to go to his room shortly after that, announcing that it was just 'TMI', leaving Kelly and Jo in comfortable silence.

"You seem to be taking things with Adam pretty well," Jo observed.

"Aye. I'm not pleased about what he's done, but I ken he must have his reasons. I've told him he's grounded for now and he's not happy to miss seeing Harry Styles in Glasgow but I think he expected it. We'll have to talk about him going back to school but I'll give us both a few days to simmer down. He's a good lad though, I'm sure we can sort it all out."

Jo made a murmur of agreement and Kelly refilled her wine glass. She'd almost forgotten about the concert in two days' time and realised they hadn't even thought what they'd do now that the Bayley cutout was gone. It would be quite nice just to go and enjoy the music without having to lug Bayley about and apologise to everyone behind them whenever she blocked their view. It's not like Harry was really going to fall madly in love with a cardboard cutout, Jo thought.

"Would you like to try a wee dram of our whisky?" Kelly was asking, and Jo happily turned her attention back to him.

Kelly brought out one of the signature butterfly-shaped bottles and she'd admired it, thinking that perhaps her moth phobia had diminished quite a lot recently. He was very proud of the design Adam had come up with, said it was a point of difference, as they were only a small distillery and you needed something to set you apart.

"If it interests you, I'll take you out to the distillery sometime and show you what we do."

He poured whisky into two beautiful heavy crystal glasses. Kelly was the perfect host, Jo thought, and, as his hand touched hers briefly when she took the whisky glass from him, really quite attractive too with his rugged looks and lovely Scottish brogue.

◇

The following morning, Jo was sitting having a cup of tea with Kelly when Bobbi wandered into the kitchen still in her robe.

"I feel so much better," she said, reaching for the teapot, as Jo and Kelly gaped at her wordlessly.

"Um, that's good to hear, Bob, but have you looked in a mirror this morning?"

Bobbi looked puzzled, but turned and went out into the hallway where there was an antique sideboard with a large mirror hanging above it. There was a loud shriek and then she came back into the room, hand over her mouth.

"Holy crap. I am *not* going anywhere like this."

Her eyes were puffy and almost closed and her lips so swollen it looked like she'd just had a collagen injection and it had gone badly wrong. Or perhaps been attacked by an angry swarm of bees.

Jo suppressed a giggle and tried to look sympathetic. "Nobody's going to see you."

"No, they're not, because I'm taking more antihistamines and staying indoors. We'll have to go to the priory tomorrow and then head back to Glasgow after that."

"I was thinking about that," Jo said, staring into her teacup. "Perhaps we should give the Glasgow concert a miss. I'd feel bad if we went and Adam wasn't able to. It's my fault his rebellious quest was brought to an end, after all. We still have the London show. That's if you don't mind us staying, Kelly?"

"I was hoping you'd stay for a bit," Kelly replied, suddenly taking great interest in buttering a plate of toast.

"I'm good with that," Bobbi replied, nabbing a piece of toast and taking a tiny nibble, gingerly trying to avoid her swollen mouth.

"Jo, if Bobbi is going to be staying indoors, perhaps you'd like to come with me out to the distillery this morning? I can easily spare a day tomorrow to drive you both out to the priory if Bobbi's feeling better."

◇

Jo loved the distillery. It was a little way out of the main village in a gorgeous old stone building with a ton of charm. Kelly had a great way of explaining the long and involved process without it sounding boring, or as if she were in kindergarten and wouldn't understand if he used big words.

For a product with only three ingredients, there were a lot of factors that affected the final product, she'd come to realise. Kelly showed her the malting room first.

It had once been a traditional malting house, he explained, where the soaked barley was spread on the floor to sprout. Now, Kelly told her, they used large rotating barrels to turn the barley and keep it warm.

"When my da was young, he used to help turn the malt. It was a bugger of a job by the sound of it and the old-timers always ended up with something called monkey's shoulder from all the repetitive shovelling," he laughed. "I was always fascinated by that. Thought it meant they got hairy arms."

They both chuckled. Kelly had a lovely laugh, Jo thought. Deep and rumbling.

The malt went into a kiln to be dried, and Kelly still used peat for heating this, explaining that that was an important part of the flavour. Jo found the smell of the malt rather lovely. Sort of like grilled bananas and strangely comforting.

"The malt is ground and turned to grist. Then we add warm water and the soluble sugars get extracted," Kelly said.

"Where does the water come from?" Jo asked, hoping that wasn't a dumb question.

"From the local Mire Loch. It's beautiful, pure and fresh," Kelly boasted. Jo loved how enthusiastic he was when he talked about his work.

"I'm envious," she confessed to him. "I wish I could do a job that I felt so much heart for."

"What work do you do yourself?"

Jo told him about her job as a proofreader. "I don't dislike it, I've always loved learning about new things," she told him, "but I don't have a passion for it."

"Aye," Kelly nodded. "Makes it much less like work when you love what you do."

Once the malt had become mash, it went into a big vessel called a turn. There, the sugars dissolved and were drawn off the bottom several times.

Jo felt like writing notes, so she could remember all the temperatures and facts involved.

Kelly led her to the washbacks next. These were big stainless steel tanks where the fermentation happened. Back in the day, Kelly told her they used to be wood, but modernisation meant they'd gone for more hygienic, easy-cleaning options. The yeast was added here, so the smell in the room was similar to a brewery. The wash then went into stills. Jo thought these were the most impressive part of the place. Two huge copper bowls, with long necks, one larger than the other. They had been hand-beaten, Kelly said, by a friend of his grandfather.

"The stills can have different neck lengths, depending on the flavour you're after. The longer the neck, the finer and lighter the whisky. A shorter, fatter neck gives a richer, fuller taste. In Scotland the distilling is done twice. Three times in Ireland, but only because they like to waste time."

Jo laughed. "Is that why the Irish add an 'e' to the word whisky as well, just more mucking around?" she asked and Kelly looked at her with amusement.

"Well, aye, I'd say you're probably right there."

"Do you do tours here? It's so interesting."

"Nae, though I'd love to," Kelly replied. "I just dinnae have the time. One day though."

This was a complicated process, the distilling part, thought Jo. But she was fascinated. Even if it hadn't been Kelly explaining it, she thought it still would have interested her.

Various parts of the liquid, all with names like low wines, foreshots and feints, were produced during this part. She really needed more time to really take it all in.

"I'd like to get into perhaps some gin as well soon," Kelly told her. "It would be a very simple process to add that to our repertoire."

Jo nodded enthusiastically. "Gin has definitely made a comeback. You could infuse flavours from local ingredients, make it a bit niche. Very trendy right now, and so many possibilities."

"Aye," Kelly agreed, smiling widely at her.

They moved on, Kelly's hand warm as it rested on the small of her back, as he led her into the barrel barn, where the oak casks were stored.

Rows and rows of barrels sat, all maturing. They used bourbon barrels, and the flavour from the charred oak gave the whisky its toffee notes rather than a sawdust taste. Casks under three years old sat on one side, since they weren't legally considered whisky yet.

"They need to age to three years and one day, before we can say they're whisky."

Jo loved that the one day was important.

"Because the oak casks are porous, they breathe. The sea air from St Abbs is vital in this aspect for the whisky flavour. About two per cent of the spirit is lost each year through evaporation," Kelly explained. "This is known as the angels' share."

Jo found that so delightful, she knew it was a fact that would stick.

Kelly drew a sample from a cask for her to try using a long

dropper. It tasted gorgeous and Jo thought she could detect a subtle taste of vanilla and honey. It felt quite intimate too, him feeding it to her, and Jo felt a weird thrill run through her.

There was a small, old stone building that was used for bottling, labelling and packing. They did all this by hand, which Jo thought was a lovely touch.

"This building was once the excise house. Back in the day, it was common for the tax man to live next to the distillery and hold the key to the distillery's 'spirit safe'. It stopped the distillery cheating on their taxes."

Kelly gave Jo a taste of various whiskies to see if she could taste the difference by age.

"Do you do public tastings?"

"I have a couple of part-time staff," 'Kelly said, "but not really anyone front of the house that can do that. Again, it's in the long-term plan though."

Jo thought how she would love to do something like that. Take people through the distillery and then have sample tastings and pairings with foods to bring out the flavours of the alcohol. Her mind raced with all the possibilities.

"This is a wonderful place," she told Kelly. "Truly, I love it. Thank you so much for showing me. I wish I could spend hours here, learning all about it."

Kelly looked pleased and a little bashful. "My pleasure," he told her. "I'm just glad I didnae bore you."

"Oh, no," Jo said firmly, "quite the opposite."

They were having such a nice day, and Jo felt a little guilty when she realised how nice it had been to have Kelly and his attention all to herself, without Bobbi along.

She took some photos to show her and sent some to Bayley on Messenger too with the comment

When in Scotland

Bayley replied back with

Looks like you're having a great time! Sam says bring back a case ♥

When they returned to the house, Bobbi was looking a little better but still very puffy. Adam had been down to the chippie to buy an enormous pile of fish and chips, which he and Bobbi had eaten. Bobbi had changed into her pyjamas, so when Kelly suggested he take them out for a drink and a meal, she declined.

"Jo, how about you? Up fer an exciting Monday night in the village?" Kelly asked, turning to her. "It's probably not even a wee bit exciting to be honest, but the pub does a reasonable surf and turf, and a pretty decent piece of haddock."

"Oh, lovely, Do I need to get changed?"

"Nae, you look bonnie as you are to me."

They put their jackets back on and walked the short distance downhill to the hotel. The Inn was a whitewashed brick building, with climbing vines around the door and a single, presently abandoned picnic table out the front. It had been built in the mid-nineteenth century, Kelly told her, and inside it was cosy, with red velvet cushioned seats and a lot of wood. A realistic-looking fire warmed the room from the chilly night air.

Kelly went to buy a pint of ale for himself and a gin for Jo. She found a seat near the stone fireplace. A row of old Toby jugs sat on the shelf behind her and she removed her outdoor wear and examined the blackboard announcing the day's specials (corn chowder and a pot pie) and encouraging folk to sign up at the bar for the Friday night pub quiz. There was an alluring prize of a round of drinks for the winning team, along with a generous meat pack, Jo noted.

It wasn't busy; there was a group of half a dozen or so men, rugged looking and windblown in cable-knit jumpers or fleece tops, worn jeans and Wellington boots laughing uproariously at a story one of them had been telling. Two men in their early twenties played darts in the corner and an older couple were enjoying a bowl of chips and a drink. The older man had given Kelly a wave in acknowledgement and one of the men from the group slapped him on the back and had a quick chat as he passed by with the drinks. She guessed this was the kind of place everybody knew everybody else. She had received a curious glance from the older woman already and the room had fallen silent for a few seconds when they'd first entered. Kelly hadn't seemed bothered and if he'd wondered what anyone was thinking about him being in the pub with an unknown woman, he hadn't shown it. But Jo did feel as though all eyes were on her as she'd made her way to the table.

Kelly handed her a menu, her glass and a bottle.

"Slàinte mhath," he said raising his.

"Cheers," Jo replied, pouring the soda into the gin.

"You've got to let me get dinner tonight, to thank you."

"You dinnae have to thank me, it's me who should be thanking you for taking care of the lad for me. He'd still be wandering the countryside if it weren't for you. What kind of a father am I that I didnae ken what my own son was doing?"

"It's the opposite with Bayley," Jo sighed. "I'm too involved in her life. Since her father and I split up I think I've lived vicariously through her a little too much. It's time I let her get on with things herself. But for the record, I don't think you should beat yourself up about Adam. He's away at school and of course you'd expect him to be safe there."

Kelly nodded. "Aye. And I cannae blame the school either. He told them he was returning to Scotland for his grandmother's funeral. Forged a letter from me and all. Children, wee toads."

"I ken what you mean," Jo nodded solemnly before grinning at him, and they both laughed.

"It's hard letting them grow up and live their own lives," Jo added. "But it *is* their life to live, not ours."

"Aye, that's true." Kelly looked thoughtful as he took a sip of his beer, and Jo studied the menu.

"Well, I cannae go past the haddock and chips. What'll it be for you, Jo?" He hadn't looked at the menu but he'd said this was about the only place you could get a meal in town, so he probably knew it by heart.

Jo said she'd have the same and watched as Kelly went up to the bar to place their order. He was wearing jeans with a fitted jumper and heavy work boots. The jeans fit him snuggly and he looked like he might have a nice arse, she thought, before she quickly turned away and studied in great depth a watercolour print on the wall of two horses grazing in a paddock before anyone caught her looking.

Their meals didn't take long to arrive, piping-hot battered haddock with a mountain of chips and coleslaw.

"There's tomato sauce *and* tartare," the woman serving told them unnecessarily, hovering beside the table. "I can get you extra lemons if you fancy them. Grow them myself, in the courtyard out back." She was looking at Kelly expectantly.

"Jo, this is Colleen, she and Mac own the pub. Colleen, my friend Jo from New Zealand."

"It's nice to meet you, Jo." Colleen held out a plump hand and Jo shook it, expecting Colleen to leave then to get back to her duties but she still lingered by the table.

"How are you, Kelly? Haven't seen you in here for a wee bit. Not since you and Finella were last in."

Kelly looked at her as he unwrapped his cutlery, a puzzled look on his face.

"I was here a couple of weeks ago?"

"Och, aye, but on your own like." She gave him an odd little pat on his shoulder and turned back to Jo.

"How are you enjoying our wee village? Will you be here for long?"

"Just a few days," Jo replied. The chips looked lovely but she didn't want to be rude and start eating them while Colleen was still standing there. She wondered what Colleen would do if she offered her one. Probably sit down and join them for the evening, she suspected.

"Well, that's lovely, it is. It's always nice to see a new face around the place." Colleen paused, waiting for a reply, but Jo just smiled back politely.

"Well, then, we'll get on with eating this fine haddock here, Colleen, before it goes cold. It looks great as usual," Kelly told her firmly.

Colleen looked a little disappointed that she couldn't stay and chat longer but nodded pleasantly and disappeared back into the kitchen.

"Sorry, the locals are … enthusiastic." He speared a chip with his fork and dipped it into the tartare sauce. "Nice people, for the most part, but a new person always makes them a wee bit curious."

They were almost finished eating when another woman popped over to say hello. Her name was Eileen and she had come to tell Kelly that their whisky stocks were a little low. Kelly explained to Jo that she owned the local bottle store, and then had to introduce them. Eileen had lingered until Kelly had suggested dessert, and then pointedly asked her to excuse them. Mac had also been over with another round of drinks on the house, and hovered till Kelly had done the introductions. Jo was both amused and frustrated that her date was being interrupted. Was it a date though? she wondered.

"Sorry about that," Kelly said again.

"Does that happen to you a lot?" Jo asked

"Ach, nae. To be honest, I've not taken many dates here, or anywhere in the village at all."

So it was a date, she thought, feeling rather fluttery and giggly at the thought.

"It took me a wee while to date after I lost Linda. It's mainly been friends and family settin' things up for me a few times, but nothing serious, mind. It's always a bit tricky when you have kids to consider." He looked at Jo and cocked his head slightly. "How about you? Have you dated much since you separated?"

Jo shook her head. "Not at all. I wasn't ready to jump back into it."

Kelly looked as if he was going to say something further but instead he nodded and offered to get them coffees.

Jo watched him as he walked back up to the bar. Not until now, she thought with a smile.

CHAPTER 26

Bayley

Her phone kept dinging with texts. She and Sam were in bed. Together. Having a little nap after some energetic shagging. They hadn't been doing much sleeping for the last couple of days. Work had been busy, and they'd been doing a lot of 'getting to know each other' in their down time.

They worked perfectly together and the chemistry was insane. Bayley had suspected they'd be good together, obviously, but Sam had turned out to be even better in the sack than she'd thought he would be. She'd thought about it a lot too.

She leant over him to reach for her mobile off the bedside table, and he snuggled into her neck, running his hand sleepily up her side and cupping a breast. Ohh, nice.

"What the fuck?"

"Wassup?" Sam mumbled.

"I've got six texts asking if I'm dead!"

Sam sat up, looking gorgeously tousled and naked. Bayley almost got distracted by his abs, but then her phone beeped again. It was Kayla. Again. Telling her to check out a link she was sending from the local news show *Seven Sharp*. What the hell?

She leant over the side of the bed and pulled her laptop out. Sam kissed the small of her back and she did a little quiver. "Cut it out," she said half-heartedly.

"You feel alive to me," Sam said, all low and sexy.

She turned and kissed him, just because she could, until her phone dinged again. Reluctantly, she opened her email and the video link.

The news presenter, Hilary Barry, came into focus. She started talking about the heartwarming story of two New Zealand sisters on a pilgrimage for their beloved daughter and niece. According to Hilary, the piece had gone viral as they followed Harry Styles around his UK shows, taking a 'piece' of their beloved one with them.

Bayley started to feel queasy. Surely not …?

The camera panned to an image of Jo and Bobbi standing in a line of mostly teenaged girls. They were holding a cardboard figure dressed in … wait. Was that her? In a red bikini?

Oh, my God.

Jo was talking to the reporter in an animated fashion and beaming with pride. Bobbi was peering over her shoulder, smiling maniacally.

Bayley could swear time stopped. She was dumbfounded.

What the hell had they done? She felt a murderous rage. A noise like a choked gargle escaped from somewhere inside her.

"Bay? What's going on?"

Wordlessly, Bayley handed her laptop to Sam and restarted the video for him. He watched it, looking sideways at her occasionally, keeping his face blank, although his lip twitched once or twice.

"Well, that's an interesting angle," he said with a small grin that faded as he looked at her face.

Bayley picked up her cell and dialled her mother, dimly aware that Sam was talking to her in a soothing voice, rubbing his hand up and down her back.

The phone rang and rang and went to voicemail. She tried again. Nothing.

"I'm sure there's a logical explanation, babe."

"Such as? I can't say I can think of a single one."

Why would they tell people she was dead? How was that going to make Harry interested? Jesus. She wasn't even that big of a fan. She'd never been a Directioner when he'd been in the band, and now her mother was going to extreme lengths to get Harry's attention. Bloody hell. What a mess.

She was only interested in one man, she thought, looking at Sam and feeling a surge of happiness wash over her, despite the anger at her mother and aunt.

She'd try her mum again later, she thought. Or Bobbi. But she was awake now, and, looking down at the tent in the sheets, so was Sam.

CHAPTER 27

Bobbi

Saffron allergy was, according to Jo, one of the least common allergies in the world. Lucky her, thought Bobbi, as she looked at herself in the mirror again. She looked like Janice bloody Dickinson's deformed twin brother, she thought miserably.

Still, when Adam woke up, after he had stopped laughing, they'd had quite a nice brunch and then played a car-racing game on his Xbox that Bobbi had been surprisingly good at, considering her lack of real-life driving skills. It had actually taken her three goes to get her driver's licence. But when it came to hooning round a virtual track, it turns out she had some skills it seemed. They'd played again briefly after their fish and chips dinner until Adam had received a couple of texts and then excused himself to his room.

Bobbi had taken the sling off, and her arm was a bit sore

now, so she took a couple of Panadol and got into bed.

She'd just been browsing Netflix looking for a new series to watch when her iPad rang with a FaceTime call from Bayley.

Bobbi's smile quickly faded when she saw her niece's face. "What's wrong?" she asked.

"Where the hell is my mother? And why isn't she answering her bloody phone?" Bayley demanded.

"She's out for dinner with Kelly, Adam's dad," Bobbi told her. "Why? What's going on?"

"You two have some explaining to do," Bayley raged. "Why the fuck are people ringing and texting me to find out if I'm dead? Why was there a cardboard cutout of *me* on *Seven Sharp*? In a goddamned fucking bikini? Honestly, Bob, I've never been so mortified *in my life*. And what the fuck is going on with your lips?"

"Oh," was all the reply Bobbi could think to give her. "I suspect maybe there was some confusion—"

"*Some* confusion," Bayley steamed. "You think?"

"Okay, calm down," Bobbi pleaded. "It wasn't intentional. We never actually said you were dead. I'm not sure where that came from. I guess the reporter may have got the wrong end of the stick."

"Well, apparently, according to Hilary Barry's report, you were taking me along as a memorial tribute to see Harry. What the hell possessed you to make a cutout of me? In my togs!"

"Yes, well, that may have been me ..." Bobbi started. "Hang

on, we were on the TV? With Hilary Barry? I just love her. What was she wearing? She has some gorgeous outfits. once she wore this fabulous—"

"Aunt Bobbi, can you concentrate? Why? Why would you do this to me? I've been dealing with Nana and Grandpa all morning too. Nana was beside herself. She said she hadn't even been told I was dead."

"Yes, right, sorry," Bobbi said, trying to sound very sorry indeed. "But it was all part of our quest to get Harry's attention. Not the dead part. We just thought you in a bikini would be an eye-catching way—"

Bayley groaned. "Oh, my God, enough. I tried to tell Mum last time we spoke that I wasn't interested. Sam and I are seeing each other now anyway and I don't need my mother to find me a husband, Harry bloody Styles or not."

"Wait, Sam?" Bobbi was a little confused. "Sam who? Not Sam, Sam. From the bar Sam?"

"Well, obviously," Bayley grumbled, but she sounded slightly less furious now. "How many Sams do you know? He's finally realised we're perfect together. We're even going out tomorrow on a date. He's taking me on a picnic." There was a chuckle from behind her that Bobbi assumed was Sam.

Bobbi was a little stunned. She and Jo had always assumed Sam was gay. Obviously, now wasn't a good time to mention *that* to Bayley. She did a bit of opening and closing of her mouth before she said, "Well, Bay, that's wonderful. I'm thrilled." She smiled at her niece, who actually looked rather dishevelled like she'd just gotten up — or something.

"Well, thanks — but you're not off the hook, Bob," Bayley said drily. "You and Mum have gone too far. I mean, the news! I'm humiliated."

"I'm so sorry, Bay, truly. We never thought it would go so far as that."

It must have been in Manchester, she thought. She remembered there was a reporter questioning people in the queue. She vaguely remembered Jo saying something about wishing her daughter could meet Harry but perhaps she hadn't mentioned Bayley was still alive.

The reporter probably hadn't wanted to upset them by asking too many questions. The New Zealand media must have picked the story up online. That would explain why so many of the girls around them had been giving them hugs, she thought now. They'd just thought that was the norm with Harry fans.

Another thought struck Bobbi then, thinking about them being on national TV. "Did they show both Jo and me? How did we look? I hope my stomach wasn't sticking out. Fancy, Hilary Barry doing a piece on us ..."

Bayley gave her a withering look and ended the call.

◇

It was overcast and the weather wasn't looking too good the next day. Kelly had some work he needed to do and then planned to return to take them to the priory in the afternoon.

Bobbi felt her face was normal enough to be seen in public, even with her lips in their plumped-up state, so they donned warm clothes and ventured out for a walk through the village. The village was a mass of old fishermen's cottages surrounded by dramatic cliffs. There was a path leading along the stone wall beside the harbour and it was rather cold. Bobbi preferred a more tropical climate but Jo said she quite liked the brisk sea air as the wind whipped their hair.

"It's bracing," she grinned at Bobbi, who pulled her beanie further down over her ears and her scarf up to cover her nose.

"I hate it when you go all Miss friggin' Pollyanna on me," Bobbi grumbled. "It's meant to be spring, but it feels like the arse end of winter."

A gust of wind blew the end of her scarf into her face and Jo laughed at her as she battled to get it under control.

There was a tiny bottle store near the pub and they called in on the way back to Kelly's to pick up a bottle of Benedictine as well as a few bottles of wine to have with dinner that night. A woman looked up from something she was doing on the computer as the doorbell buzzed. They were the only customers in the store and the streets had been quiet. Bobbi wondered whether they'd been the only customers of the day so far.

"Ah, Kelly's friend — Jo, was it?" the lady said, perking up and looking at them curiously.

"And you have someone else with you?" Bobbi thought that was stating the obvious. She was standing there in full view, not hiding behind a shelf of spirit bottles.

"This is my sister Bobbi," Jo told Eileen, and then turned to Bobbi. "I met Eileen at the pub last night."

"You were having a bit of dinner with Kelly," Eileen stated beadily.

Bobbi used all her restraint and managed to not roll her eyes.

"I was," was Jo's reply.

"Ach, well, I hope you enjoyed yourselves. How can I help you?"

Eileen didn't stock any New Zealand wines, which wasn't much of a surprise, and hadn't in the thirty years she'd owned the shop. Bobbi told her she'd send her some information about a supplier if she was interested and they picked out a few bottles of a Chilean red that sounded good and a couple of a nice chianti. They told Eileen about their quest for Uncle Bill and she plucked a bottle of Benedictine from the shelf for them.

Eileen thought she vaguely recalled Uncle Bill, but it turned out she was thinking of an entirely different person who had drowned at sea forty years beforehand and was named Gordon. They finally got away and sang 'Come on Eileen' all the way back up the hill to Kelly's house.

◇

"I feel like we should dress for the occasion," Bobbi said, when they arrived back and had gone into their room to get changed for the visit to the priory. "It's only fitting for a memorial. Did you bring anything special?"

Unlike Bobbi, Jo actually had mostly black clothes anyway. She put on black trousers and a black merino jumper, which was a lot more suitable for the weather than Bobbi's sparkly black dress. Bobbi was certain that Uncle Bill would appreciate the effort though, besides, she'd lugged it all the way over here, so she put the dress on along with the red parka she'd been wearing earlier. Jo put the Benedictine into her bag with the sparkly cigar box of ashes and the letter from Uncle Bill.

Kelly drove them the short way to the priory and Bobbi was pleased to see the car park was empty when they arrived. She checked her lips again in the mirror one last time and added a swipe of red lipstick for good measure. They got out and entered the priory from the east, walking down a path and through a large freestanding arch where some columns stood in a state of ruin. The church itself was a large oblong building of pink-hued stones. The upper half of its windows looked boarded over. It was a pretty impressive, imposing structure. It felt steeped in history.

Around them were more ruins and headstones and derelict old walls. Bobbi glanced at the sky, grey and ominous, certain she had just felt a few droplets of rain.

They wandered around the main building, taking it all in. Two of the walls on the north and east were incredibly ornate, while the other walls to the south and west were strikingly plain in contrast.

Kelly told them a bit of history about the site as they

walked. It had been established by Saint Æbbe in 635 and was used by monks and nuns, until a fire destroyed the monastery.

"Rumour has it this was 'Divine retribution' for some very un-monk-like behaviour. It was rebuilt and used just by the nuns after that. Then the Benedictines."

As Kelly explained its history, it seemed it had just been destroyed and rebuilt continuously over the centuries. By Vikings, and by King John of England, and then set fire to again by its prior William Drax to cover up his stealing.

"It was finally destroyed in the 1650s by Oliver Cromwell."

"Man, you guys have way better history stories than us," Bobbi lamented.

A lot of the area was still just ruins. Very old, historic ruins. The grounds, however, had been turned into community gardens, which were lovely, and practical too.

It was a fascinating place, and in better weather it would have been great to spend some time exploring.

But the wind was getting up and so they sheltered near the church and Bobbi opened the envelope containing the handwritten letter they'd been instructed to read at this moment.

She suddenly felt all emotional and handed the letter to Kelly.

"Would you mind reading it out?"

Kelly cleared his throat and started to read. With his accent, they could almost imagine Uncle Bill was speaking to them.

Dear Roberta and Josephine,

Well, lassies, it would seem like I've carked it if you're reading this.

Popped ma clogs, kicked the bucket.

You were like children to Avis and me, girlies, and so firstly I want to say thank you.

I know I was a crotchety old bugger sometimes, and especially after I lost Avis, God rest her soul, so I appreciate that you were kind to me.

I've left you both some money. It's not a lot, mind, but I hope you use it for something frivolous and fun. Spend it unwisely, will you? Life can be short.

If you've opened this, I'm hopeful it's because you're at Coldingham Priory. I grew up in a house down the road and I have fond memories of the place, running wild and free with my good mate, Patrick McFadden.

So, if you've got the ashes, do me the first favour, and throw me into the wind there. Let me run free again around the place. Anywhere you think suitable is fine. And have a wee dram of Benedictine for me, will you? I've always loved the idea of the monks making it and having a wee tipple sometimes when no one was looking.

So this leads me to my second request, and back to Patrick.

When we were bairns, my parents weren't rich by any means, and we didn't have spare cash for extras. Father's Day was coming up, and I didn't have a gift for my da. One day, at Patrick's, I saw his grandfather's pocket watch on a dresser in his room, and, I'm ashamed to say, I took it to give to my da.

Of course, I never did. His grandad noticed it was missing, and I knew they'd recognise it if I regifted it. I never confessed, and I was too scared to try and return it. So I buried it.

I know it probably doesn't matter now, but it's been a yoke around my neck all these years.

So I'd like to ask you both to find the watch and return it to Paddy. I buried it beside the grave of my own grandad (and my namesake) William Anderson. It's on the left of his headstone, not too deep as I recall.

He's buried on the west side of the priory and the grave next to him is a big winged angel. He died in 1952.

I'd like to have a little piece of Avis come with me, so you'll find our wedding rings in the envelope too (if my solicitor hasn't turned out to be a thieving bastard).

Please dig up the watch. It's in a small liniment tin. Then put the rings back in there.

You're probably thinking I'm a silly old man, but Avis was a good woman, and I'm hoping to join her upstairs. So I'm dotting my i's and crossing my t's.

I'll rest easier knowing you've done this for me.

Thank you, my girls, and buy yourselves some lollies, won't you?

It's been magic.

Love, Uncle Bill.

Inside the envelope were two rings and two old, out-of-circulation fifty-cent pieces. Jo pulled out a tissue pack and handed one to Bobbi. They dabbed their eyes and Bobbi blew her nose loudly. All of them had a swig or two from the liquor bottle to do a final toast to Uncle Bill. No one had remembered to bring glasses.

Then the rain really started.

They waited a while to see if it would stop, but it only got heavier. The cloud seemed to have become even more ominous and a lot darker.

They discussed coming back another day, but Bobbi had spotted a trowel in one of the medicinal gardens earlier, and had also seen an angel monument as they walked past the graves, so at her insistence they split up, with Jo and Kelly taking half the ashes each and spreading them around at will. She volunteered to get the watch and meet them back at the car as soon as possible. "I'll text you if I have any issues," she said, pocketing the rings and flipping up the hood of her jacket before trudging off with a wave. If it was too hard to find the bloody tin, she'd say she'd tried and leave it at that.

She squelched her way to the herb garden, wishing for a torch, but found the trowel quite easily. Then off she set to the gravesites, wiping the rain off her face and regretting immensely the dress and heeled boots.

As she walked through the grounds, she found herself in a section filled with what seemed to be children's graves. She slowed her pace and read the names on the white crosses as she went. Some were older, the writing more difficult to read. But all were babies that someone had lost, and Bobbi thought of her own child as she read the names and dates. A newer cross caught her eye. On the inscription was a single date — the same as her own child's beginning and end. She paused, feeling herself well up at the loss, still lingering inside her. She looked up at the sky, rain hitting her cheeks, mingling with her tears. When she looked back, a small carnelian-hued bird was perched on the cross, its head cocked as if watching her. It chirped several notes, sweet and melodious, and Bobbi felt a warmth spread through her at the sound. It fluttered its wings, lifting up, and off, flying past Bobbi without fear, so close she felt the air move near her head. An odd feeling of peace settled over her as it left and Bobbi kept moving, feeling like she could leave a little bit of her grief behind as she went.

The grave was surprisingly easy to find and she gave herself a mental pat on the back as she knelt down and started to dig. The wet soggy ground made the soil relatively easy to move and soon she had uncovered quite an area. It was hard to work out how deep to go, but she went about fifteen or twenty centimetres down, and on her third hole, hit something metal. Success! The tin came loose quite easily and she wiped it on her coat before prying it open. Inside was the watch, looking a bit worse for wear. She doubted it even worked, but she scooped it up, and swapped it out for the rings before returning the tin to the hole.

She'd made a bit of a mess, she realised, so she set to work trying to even out the ground and fill it all in as well as she could. The rain was really pelting down, causing rivulets of mud to run back into the holes she had dug, and it had started to get quite dark. To be honest, it was a little bit freaky being out here by herself. She started to hum one of Harry's songs and then realised it was 'Two Ghosts' and not the best choice for the occasion. If Jo jumped out from somewhere and scared the crap out of her, she'd be so pissed. She'd done that once when they stayed at a haunted hotel in New Orleans and Bobbi had nearly peed her pants.

"Don't you go trying to trick me, Josephine," she said out loud. "I'm not scared and I'll know it's you." She hoped she didn't sound scared. She also hoped no one else could hear her talking to what was probably thin air.

The water was puddling up even more and flooding over her boots. The rain battered the back of her legs, soaking her stockings. She shovelled faster. The wind had picked up, so she didn't hear the noise of footsteps behind her until there was a loud cough and a tap on her shoulder. A figure loomed behind her in a long, flowing trench coat, holding a flashlight, too tall to be Jo or Kelly. Bobbi screamed.

CHAPTER 28

Jo

Jo had walked further than she realised. There was a lovely copse of trees she'd decided would be a nice final resting place for Uncle Bill, while Kelly had gone to sprinkle his half of the ashes in an open field nearby. It was a popular picnic spot in summer, he told her, possibly her uncle had picnicked there himself. It had started to rain heavily by the time Jo had finished, so pulling her coat around her she went to find Kelly so they could make their way back to the car. She must have made a wrong turn and it had begun to get dark amongst the trees. Water dripped from her hood and unpleasantly down her neck. Was that a scream? Jo stopped and listened for a second but decided she was just being stupid. It was just the wind, she told herself, but she picked up her pace and eventually managed to find her way out of the wooded area, relieved to see Kelly coming towards her.

"I thought you'd got lost in there. Come on, let's get back," he called, and they made their way back to Bobbi and the car. But Bobbi wasn't there. There was no sign of her at all.

"She must be still at the graves. I'll go and tell her to forget about the watch," Jo decided. Her teeth were chattering. "At least we would have tried."

Kelly reached over and absently plucked out a couple of stray leaves that had got caught in Jo's hair while she'd be rambling through the trees.

"You get in the car and try to get warm, I think there's a blanket in the back. I'll go and find Bobbi." He threw Jo the keys. "Here, put the heater on."

Jo hopped into the driver's seat and turned the key. The engine seemed to be dead. She fiddled with the buttons a bit but, being an unfamiliar car and not hers to fiddle with, soon gave up and awkwardly climbed into the passenger seat, pulling the blanket from the back seat around her.

Kelly was gone a while and came back alone, completely drenched and looking worried.

"There's no sign of her. I looked up by the church in case she'd gone there to shelter but it's locked and there's no one around. Perhaps she's gone down the road to the Inn."

They'd passed the Inn on the way to the priory and Jo thought that was quite likely. She felt a bit pissed off that Bobbi hadn't even bothered to text her.

"I think the battery might be flat," Jo told him, still shivering despite the blanket.

Kelly got in and tried to start the car. The battery was indeed completely flat.

"Shite."

He tried again.

"Bloody Bobbi," Jo exclaimed, remembering suddenly. "I'll bet she left the bloody light on when she was checking her lips in the mirror. Vain tart."

"The Inn's only a wee walk, shall we go and check there?" Kelly pulled out the bottle of Benedictine from where he'd tucked it into his coat and grinned at her. He seemed cheerful despite the storm, and it wasn't even his uncle or his sister who had caused them to be in this mess. Jo admired that in a man.

"A wee dram for the road?" he asked, raising one eyebrow as he opened the bottle.

"Go on then, after you," Jo replied, smiling a little.

◇

They were completely drenched when they finally pushed through the doors, dripping water all over the foyer as they shed their coats. They weren't much drier underneath, thought Jo, looking at Kelly's top sticking to his firm chest. She hoped hers wasn't clinging quite as much. She attempted to pull the soggy material away from her body, then gave up. She was glad she hadn't bothered with makeup. Her hair was hanging limply against her cheek and rain had run down her pant leg into her now squelchy shoes.

Bobbi wasn't at the Inn either but there was a man drinking a pint of ale at the bar who overheard them explaining their predicament to the innkeeper. He'd just come from out near the priory and had seen a police car up near the graveyard. A woman in a red coat had got into the wagon with Barney, the chief constable. Jo felt a bit better. Trust Bobbi to manage to wrangle a ride home, but she was still a bit miffed that she hadn't bothered to tell them. She pulled out her phone to call.

"You cannae make a call from here," the innkeeper told her. "There's nae service and the phone lines are all down. The road is flooded too so you won't be able to get help for your car in a hurry."

"So we can't get back into town?" Jo asked, and he shook his head.

"Nae, the road into town is completely out. You'll have to wait it out, I'm afeard. I can bring you both a bowl of broth and some of me wife's homemade bread, if you'd like it?"

He told them there was another couple staying there, but luckily the Inn had two rooms and they'd be welcome to the second one. Jo snuck a glance at Kelly to check his reaction to sharing a room, but he seemed fine, quite cheerful even. Wasn't he lovely?

They agreed, neither mentioning they weren't a couple. The innkeeper led the way up a narrow staircase to the room. It looked like it hadn't been redecorated since the 1970s, but had a shower and hot water which, at this stage, was all that mattered. There was a bed with a candlewick bedspread and a large armchair which Kelly was eyeing up, probably gauging how comfortable it would be to sleep on. The room was cosy and warm thanks to a large oil heater. The innkeeper had given them extra blankets to wrap themselves in and there were robes in the wardrobe, he told them.

"You have the first shower," Kelly gallantly told Jo. "And then we'll have some soup. I hope Bobbi won't be worried about what's happened to us. I tried to get hold of Adam but it's true, there's not any service."

"She's probably sitting at home with her feet up and a glass of wine," Jo muttered uncharitably.

"Aye, perhaps she'll send out a search party and they'll come and rescue us," Kelly added. He had an expression on his face Jo couldn't quite read.

◇

After showering and draping their clothes around the room as best as they could to dry, they felt a lot more comfortable. Wrapped in robes and warm blankets, they went back downstairs and sat by the fire to eat their soup and then sipped glasses of the remaining Benedictine.

"Here's to your Uncle Bill," Kelly toasted, once again.

"Lover of adventures," Jo said, raising her glass.

"If this isnae one, I don't know what is." They clinked glasses.

Jo adjusted her dressing gown, hoping it wasn't gaping.

"I'm so sorry we've put you to all this bother." She did genuinely feel bad about that, but she was warm now and the alcohol was helping. There was something about sitting by a roaring fire, a proper one, the embers crackling and with the wind and rain battling each other outside. And Kelly was really lovely company.

Kelly waved a hand dismissively.

"'Tis nothin' at all. In fact, I haven't had as much fun in years. After the accident and Linda died, I didn't do much but work and worry about the kids."

"I'm so sorry you lost your wife like that. It must have been an awful time for you all."

"Aye," Kelly agreed, "and it was hard on Hannah and Adam. Maybe I shouldn't have sent them away to school. They could have gone into Edinburgh like the other local kids, but I thought it would be best if they got away and just got on with things. A fresh start for them, I suppose."

"Well, if Hannah's anything like Adam, you've produced lovely kids. A credit to you both."

There was a sudden crack of lightning that made Jo jump and then the rumble of thunder a few seconds later.

"Well, I dinnae think it's going to get better. That search party won't be coming for us."

At that moment the lights flickered and the power went out. The innkeeper's wife bustled out with candles, which didn't add much brightness but cast a pretty glow around the room.

"Ah well," Kelly said, pouring another slug of liqueur into their glasses. "What else are you to do?"

He got up and put another log on the fire and Jo found herself admiring his bare legs, visible from under the robe, and thinking about things she hadn't thought about in years. She quickly picked up her glass and sipped her drink to distract herself. Jesus. What was wrong with her? Why was she suddenly thinking about the things she was thinking about?

She and Marcus hadn't had sex, or even kissed, in years and she'd thought she didn't mind that. Turns out she was wrong.

◇

By the time they'd finished the bottle it was getting late and they made their way up the narrow stairs to their room, Kelly carrying a candle like a beacon to lead the way.

There was a slightly awkward moment as they stood, neither looking at the other, but instead focused on the bed dominating the room.

"I'll take the chair," Kelly offered as he moved to take extra blankets and a pillow from the wardrobe.

"Kelly, don't be silly, the bed is enormous," Jo announced firmly. "I'm sure we won't even need to make a pillow wall down the middle." They both laughed awkwardly.

"Well, if you're sure," Kelly said. "I'll try my best to be an honourable gentleman." They got into bed, robes still on. He blew out the candle and they lay in a slightly awkward silence for a few seconds.

Kelly's voice seemed even deeper in the dark.

"I cannae think of anyone I'd rather be here with. It certainly beats the time as a lad I got stuck in Dundee and had to share a room with my Great-aunt Gladys."

Jo laughed.

"You have such a lovely laugh," Kelly said, and there was something in his voice that gave Jo the courage to reply, "You know, you don't need to be too much of an honourable gentleman, Kelly, if you don't want to be."

She wasn't sure after that which of them lunged first.

CHAPTER 29

Bobbi

It wasn't the initial arrest for grave-digging that irked her, after all she could see that her actions had looked suspicious. They hadn't charged her in the end, once she'd explained why she was in the priory cemetery with a trowel.

Nor was it having to spend the night in the tiny police cell on the little narrow bed. Nope. Even if it had been a bit mortifying, it wasn't so bad when they got to the station where she took off her coat and sat down for questioning, to have one of the other officers comment that she must be new to the beat. It had taken her a few minutes to realise he thought she was a local hooker. But that wasn't the bit that she was mad at. Well, not much. Especially when he found her a towel to dry her hair.

Finally she managed to set everything straight, and Barney asked her a few questions such as where she was from, what she did for work, her age, where she was staying, and so on. Once that was done, Bobbi quite enjoyed time with the squad, talking and playing poker. She tried to pull a con on them, saying she'd never played before, in the hopes of cleaning up. Turns out, even though she had played a fair bit, she was still crap at the game. No poker face.

One of the lads rustled up some crisps and peanuts, and they all had several warm mugs of tea. The station had its own generator, so when the storm really hit, they still had lights and heat and it was cosy. It hadn't been a bad night. She'd certainly had a lot worse.

No, the thing that made her really grumpy was the next morning when they signed her off and gave her a copy of the paperwork. There, in Barney's tidy block letters under Occupation, were the words 'DRAG QUEEN'.

She consoled herself with the thought that it was her puffy lips and not her broad shoulders (swimmer's shoulders, Doreen always said).

After she'd been released, a cute young officer kindly dropped her back to Kelly's since he and Jo were too busy sorting his flat battery to offer to pick her up from the clink. When they finally returned, looking a little guilty for, she assumed, leaving her to be arrested and not bailing her out, she told them her grievance. Jo and Kelly, however, had found the whole thing most amusing. They'd laughed far too loudly and for far too long for Bobbi's liking.

Still, after a coffee, shower and some porridge, she could

sort of see the funny side. Sort of.

Kelly left to get to work soon after he and Jo got back. It was mid-morning, after all. He had been apologetic about leaving them to their own devices but Bobbi assured them they would work on finding Patrick McFadden and he didn't need to stay. She commented to Jo that she hoped they weren't overstaying their welcome and perhaps they should cook him dinner that night to thank him for his hospitality. Jo readily agreed, which was just as well, since Bobbi was no chef. Her only kitchen skill was in assembling cheese platters. And cocktails. Jo, however, was a pretty damn good cook. Probably where Bayley had gotten her talent.

Jo was quite impressed Bobbi had actually found the watch and gave it a bit of a clean-up, although it still seemed like a bit of a waste of time tracking down its owner. It didn't look like it was worth anything since it hadn't fared well in the ground for almost seventy years. It certainly wasn't working. Still, they'd do what Bill had requested, if they could.

The internet was still down from the storm, so they decided to wander into the village and see if anyone remembered Uncle Bill's mate. Hopefully he still lived there and they could get this done and dusted quickly.

They put on their coats and hats and wandered down the cobbled stone paths to the pub.

The local was surprisingly busy for a weekday. Mostly fishermen, they figured, forced to wait out the storm. It was still drizzling, but the pub was warm and inviting.

There was an older gentleman with an impressive moustache wearing a black apron standing behind the bar as they approached, who Jo told her was Mac, the owner. They ordered a gin and soda each to be polite before asking him if he knew Patrick McFadden, friend of their Uncle William.

"Aye, to be sure, wasn't he the chap, lived up near the priory?"

They nodded eagerly. "I remember him, he and his sister were right tearaways," he reminisced. "And that Bill. Always into mischief."

"Here, Pete," he called out to a grey-bearded bloke playing darts, "didn't your neighbour's girl marry that Paddy bloke up the hill?"

Pete wandered over, smelling of brine and tobacco, and proceeded to tell them a long-winded story about someone called Beth that he'd always fancied himself. She had briefly been married to Patrick, it transpired. Bobbi started to feel quite hopeful of tracking him down.

Another fisherman, Connor, joined them, wearing a cosy-looking jumper with leather patches on the elbows. He had a warm smile, and a weather-beaten face. They discussed Beth and how she'd ended up running off with the vicar's son, never to be seen again. Patrick had been devastated, never married again, said Connor's wife Mary who'd joined them at the bar.

"Lucky bugger," muttered Mac under his breath as he mopped down the bar.

There was another story about Beth that Mary's friend Joan supplied about a rumoured affair with the bloke who came round with his anvil to sharpen knives. There was a heated discussion between Pete and Joan then about Beth's virtue and the validity of such gossip.

It was getting a little off track and confusing by now but Bobbi managed to interject eventually and ask where Patrick lived.

"Oh, he were years up at the top house," said Mac.

"Aye, but then did he not go to live down the ways a bit, when he were grown?" Connor pondered.

"Did he not move in with his sister after that?" Mary questioned, and they all agreed.

"Aye, he and the sister, were her name Heather? They lived in the wee grey cottage, next to the McTavish family," Pete confirmed.

"Ach but wasn't that Grahame McTavish a dish, so, Mary?" giggled Joan.

Joan's husband James, a ruddy-faced man with a bulbous nose, snorted derisively. "Ach, he were nae as dishy as me but, were he, pet?" Joan patted his leg fondly while she rolled her eyes at Mary to the right.

"'Twas Heather. The sister. I remember her dog, funny little fella with only one eye. It were always after hanging round the butchers' down by the dock hoping for a scrap," Pete said fondly, and they all agreed that it was a wee beaut of a dog.

Bobbi tried to swing the conversation back to the cottage after the discussion led on to who owned the butchers' back then. (Mac said the Smiths and Connor was sure it was the Donaldsons.)

"So, the grey cottage you think, next to the McTavish house?"

"Aye," said Mary, "were just the two of them, they got on well, and you'd oft see them round, with that wee dog — Scruffy were its name." There was a chorus of agreement that indeed, it was Scruffy. Although Mac's wife Colleen said she thought it was Buffy, but was ignored.

"Great," said Jo a little tiredly, "and where might that cottage be so we can drop off this watch of his?"

There was a collective hush in the room and then Connor replied; "Well, it's only a wee ways, but nae point going round there, lassies. Paddy's been dead for some time now."

For fuck's sake, thought Bobbi, this was like bleeding *Fawlty Towers*.

Jo sighed and pressed her fingers to her temples. "So," she said slowly and patiently, "Patrick McFadden is deceased?"

"Och, aye," the patrons agreed in unison. "Has bin for years," added Connor.

There was a strained silence until another bloke who'd been sitting at the table nearby, sipping a port, piped up, "His sister's alive but."

Almost an hour later, they had finally established that Heather McFadden was in fact alive and residing in a rest home in the next town over.

Filled with hope to end this wild goose chase, and fuelled by more gin, they'd eventually been offered a ride in Seamus's pick-up truck and dropped off at the Shady Elms Care Facility.

◇

Inside it was overly warm and smelt like an unpleasant mix of urine, bleach and boiled cabbage.

Bobbi and Jo approached the front desk and located a middle-aged woman called Ruth, sitting behind a large vase of purple hydrangeas, who gave them instructions on where to find Heather. "It will be nice for her to have visitors," she beamed. "She doesnae get many. Are you relatives?"

"No, just friends of sorts," Jo replied, and they wandered down the hallway into a sitting room. There were a few residents sitting around in armchairs, mostly looking blankly at a TV with Andre Bocelli crooning away on the screen.

One woman was rocking quietly in a chair, humming to a plastic doll she had swaddled in her arms. Another was colouring in a picture with fat crayons.

A caregiver in navy scrubs was slowly feeding a frail-looking gentleman some soup. She looked up as they entered and Bobbi asked her if she could point out Heather.

She indicated a woman in the far corner, wearing a formal dinner jacket over the top of a yellow sweater and navy leisure pants. She had mismatched shoes and a fascinator perched on her head, feather sticking up at a jaunty angle.

Beside her on the seat was a bright-pink evening clutch.

Heather, they were not surprised to discover, quite obviously didn't know who they were. She didn't know who she was either. She was very confused. Dementia, they assumed. She told Jo she was off to the theatre and then, a few minutes later, that she needed to get to work and could they mind Buffy. They both took turns trying to make conversation with her, explaining why they were there, but eventually gave up. She did seem to perk up when they mentioned Patrick's name, but it was hard to tell if it had really registered. Bobbi held out the watch to her and Heather was quick to snatch it up, opening her purse and popping it in, with a sneaky glance around to ensure nobody had seen her. Then she pulled out and offered Bobbi and Jo a pre sucked Oddfellow, which they politely declined.

There wasn't much left to do or say at that point, and as the staff started to round the residents up for an afternoon singalong, they said their goodbyes and left. It was unlikely the watch meant a thing to Heather, but it was as good as they were going to get in the way of fulfilling Uncle Bill's wishes, so it would have to do.

◇

They caught a cab to the nearest supermarket and purchased some bits and pieces for dinner. Jo was planning on making a lemon pasta, with pavlova for dessert. They made a second stop to purchase some nice cheeses and olives at a local deli, before making their way back to Kelly's house, thankful that they still had most of their own marbles.

CHAPTER 30

Adam

"Don't blame me for falling ..." Adam sang as he washed his hair. He was feeling surprisingly cheerful today, despite the fact he and his da still hadn't really spoken. Having Bobbi and Jo here had definitely helped delay that and had most likely given Kelly the chance to calm down a bit.

He was actually thinking he might sit his da down tonight for a chat. Man to man. It was time.

He'd outline his plan, tell him what he wanted to do. He was willing to go back to school for the rest of year twelve, but wanted to look at a music school or a course for the following year. And, he decided, he'd tell his da he was gay. It was definitely time.

This confidence had come about, he knew, from Thomas.

It had been late last night and Thomas had sent him a text, asking him if he was okay, and saying he was sorry about his gran.

He wondered briefly who Thomas had asked to get his number.

For a while, he lay on his bed trying to formulate a reply. Eventually, he'd texted back and asked if he could call instead.

They'd spoken for about fifteen minutes. Adam had confessed that his gran was alive and well, and told him he'd been at Harry's concerts. Thomas was dead jealous and Adam plucked up the nerve to ask if he wanted to go to Harry's London show with him. He'd have to plead his da to go, he thought now. Shit. But he'd have to head back to London for school and hopefully his da would be stoked he was going back. It would be a waste not to use the tickets.

Thomas, as it turned out, already had a ticket for the same night. They arranged to meet there. It was exciting and Adam felt the familiar nervous excitement he got whenever he thought about Thomas.

Thomas has started at his school mid-year. He'd walked into Adam's music class, looking nervously around at all the faces, and Adam's breath had caught as they made eye contact, then his dick had perked up too. He had to casually pull his shirt out of his pants to cover himself, and hoped Mr Loch didn't call on him for anything that required him to stand up.

Thomas sat in front of him and even from the back he looked fit. His dark hair was shaved up the back, and around his pale neck was a thin, silver necklace. Adam found himself constantly imagining running a finger up the nape of his neck. He had to think about old ladies' undies to settle himself down.

Later that week, Adam's band played at assembly and he'd almost missed his cue when he noticed Thomas was looking intently at him, a small smile playing on his lips.

After that, it was like Adam had a spidey sense every time Thomas was near him. His heart would pound and the hairs on his neck would rise. He saw him around school a lot, and he found himself looking for him, watching him. He was nice too. Not just good looking. Kind to the younger kids and always cheerful in the mornings.

They were only in two classes together, music and science. Adam was conflicted about that. He wished he was in his PE class too, just so he could see him in his gym kit, but also glad. It was bad enough getting a boner when he sat at the science lab tables, let alone while they were in the gymnasium where it would be harder to hide.

Thomas was pretty open about his sexuality at school. He'd been given a bit of ribbing from a couple of dickhead guys his first year there. He hadn't let it bother him too much. He told Adam about coming out to his parents and his mates. And he said something to Adam that hit home. "If you feel like you can't be you, because you're not being honest about who you are, then how can anyone know you and like you for you, including yourself?"

◇

As he stepped out of the shower to get dressed, Adam felt glad things had happened like they did. He'd get to spend the rest of the school year with Thomas and hopefully take some ownership over his life. He went over to his laptop and fired it up. Thomas had promised to send notes from a science lab he'd missed, and some course notes too. Adam had a bit of catching up to do, to show his da he was taking things seriously. He put Harry on the speakers and sang along as he studied.

◇

Kelly came home quite cheerful and seemed very pleased about the dinner Jo had prepared. Bobbi opened a bottle of wine and Kelly raved about Jo's 'mad skills' as they ate, making Jo blush. Adam was very helpful and set the table, and also cleared it, before offering to do the dishes again.

When he got back to the lounge, Kelly had made special coffees and everyone looked very relaxed.

"Da," he started, clearing his throat. "I was wondering if we could, umm, talk."

Jo went to stand, saying; "Oh, we can give you some privacy." Kelly reached out his hand and pushed her gently back down onto the couch next to him. His hand stayed resting on her thigh as she sat. "I dinnae think that's necessary, is it, Adam?"

Adam thought about it briefly. It would work in his favour, he figured, to have Jo and Bob there if things got heated. He got the feeling they'd be supportive and would take his side. But in the end he didn't need it.

He told his da his plan to go back and finish the school year . Kelly looked thrilled and said as much. Then Adam mentioned the possibility of doing a music course. Kelly thought about it a bit before saying that was a definite option and Adam should look at what entry requirements they all had so they could look at them together.

Adam was very pleased. He decided since his da was in a good mood to also bring up Harry's London concert and pointed out he'd have to go back to London anyway for school.

Kelly was less sure about that, but Bobbi pointed out that they would be there too and happy to supervise.

"I could stay with Aunty Jen," he added.

Adam told them a little bit about Thomas, and how he was hoping to meet him in London.

"Get back to me with your plans, and we'll talk about that then, shall we?" said Kelly.

There was a lull. "Anything else, bud?"

Okay, this was it.

"The thing is, Da," Adam started. Then paused. "The thing is—" he said again.

He looked down at his feet and rubbed them backwards and forwards against the rug. He'd had a whole speech planned in his mind, but it had gone blank.

"Well, I'm sorta gay," he blurted out. He didn't want to look up. "I mean, not sorta. I am. Gay, that is." He gulped.

Kelly gave a funny little laugh under his breath and Adam finally looked at him. He was smiling softly at him.

"Well, aye, Adam," he said. "I sorta knew that."

He reached across Jo and ruffled Adam's hair tenderly.

"Your mother and I kinda figured that out years ago, son." Adam felt a lump in his throat, and tears welled up.

"Really?" he croaked out.

"Aye, and gay or not, dinnae matter a jot to me. I hope you know that."

Jo did a little quiet sniffle beside him that made Adam laugh. He stood up at the same time as Kelly and they hugged.

"Love ya, son," Kelly whispered in his ear.

"You too," he replied huskily.

Adam went to bed that night feeling like a weight had been lifted. He texted Thomas

Told Da

and couldn't help the wide smile that spread across his face at his reply.

Cool. now u can be u

Life was good.

CHAPTER 31

Jo

Jo lay in bed that night thinking about the day. It had been a good one. Quite productive. When she'd woken at the Inn that morning Kelly wasn't there so that had made it less awkward as she showered and dressed in yesterday's clothes, which were still slightly damp. She'd found Kelly downstairs where he'd organised someone to give him a jump start and had arrived back with the car just in time for them to have some breakfast together.

They had clearly been avoiding looking each other in the eye and Jo had tried not to grin like a loon, but it wasn't as uncomfortable as it could have been. They didn't talk much on the short drive back to town and arrived home to find Bobbi who, it turned out, hadn't been merely offered a ride back from the priory but had nearly been arrested for grave-digging.

Jo didn't even go off at Bobbi for leaving the lights on in the car and causing the battery to go flat in the first place. It had all worked out pretty well in the end, she decided, and she didn't want Bobbi to ask too many questions about where they had been for the night. She simply told Bobbi they'd had to walk to an inn where they'd waited out the storm. Kelly didn't say a word about it either and gave her a secretive little grin and raised his eyebrows suggestively when Bobbi wasn't looking, before he headed off to do some work.

After Jo had showered and changed, she and Bobbi had gone to find Uncle Bill's friend Paddy McFadden and they'd met some interesting characters along the way, but Jo had been a little distracted thinking about the previous night.

It was hard to tell how Kelly felt about it, she thought now. Did he just see it as a one-off thing? Because she really felt she didn't want it to be. From what she'd seen so far he didn't seem the type to drag random women, albeit willingly, into bed, shag them and discard them, but, who knew? Still — he really didn't seem like a player. It had been a really good night. She gave a little shiver of pleasure thinking about it.

Kelly had been overly complimentary about the meal she'd made. She was surprised that Bobbi hadn't noticed. But then Adam had made his announcement to Kelly about being gay so she guessed that had taken the focus off her and Kelly.

She'd met him as she came out of the bathroom after brushing her teeth and he'd looked like he was about to say something, or maybe even snog her, but at that moment

Bobbi opened the bedroom door and they'd jumped even further apart.

◇

Now, Jo plumped her pillow and half listened as Bobbi made suggestions for the following day, but her mind wasn't really on the conversation.

It was on a lovely Scotsman just a short way down the hall.

CHAPTER 32

Bobbi

The next day the weather had vastly improved so Bobbi and Jo took a cab to Eyemouth for a look at Gunsgreen House.

As it transpired, their driver was none other than Connor from the pub, so they filled him in on their previous day finding Heather as they drove. He was helping out his son, who was the owner of the cab, but wasn't feeling well. He arranged to drive them around for the morning and was happy waiting in the car for them, reading his book, while they looked around the museum.

It turned out to be a fascinating house. Built in 1753, it was designed by the now-famous architect John Adams for a local merchant named John Nisbet, who was also a smuggler.

There was a large cellar and hidden tunnels that led directly to the sea where Nisbet received deliveries of contraband by ship. Tobacco, brandy and tea were smuggled into the house to avoid the high taxes.

Upstairs there was a hidden room, in case smugglers got trapped ashore. Jo and Bobbi had particularly loved the tea chute hidden cleverly in the walls of the house.

After they'd spent about an hour exploring, Connor drove them into the town to look at the shops and buy some gifts.

It wasn't until Jo mentioned getting something for Bayley that Bobbi remembered she hadn't told her about the Face-Time conversation with her niece, and that she and Jo had been on TV.

Jo was also a Hilary Barry fan so they sat and had a coffee and tried to google and see what was actually said, and how they'd looked, with no luck. Doreen would have taped it, they hoped.

Jo had been mainly concerned about how mad Bayley was until Bobbi got to the bit where she and Sam were now dating.

"Wow," Jo said quietly. "I thought he was gay."

"Me too," Bobbi said. "Totally."

"In fact, I'm sure you told me that," Jo accused. "So much for the fabulous gaydar you claim to have."

They laughed and after a while decided that, now they knew he wasn't gay, Sam and Bayley together made perfect sense.

"I guess we have to give up on the Harry Styles marriage now," lamented Bobbi.

"Yes, well, I'd sort of come to my senses about that already I think. I got a bit fixated on the idea. Took my mind off Marcus, I guess." She picked up her cup. "I really do feel a bit sorry for Harry. He has a lot of people wanting to marry him, I'd imagine. I would have had adorable grandchildren though."

"There could be worse things than the whole world being in love with you, I guess," Bobbi said. "We *are* still going to his last concert though, right?"

Jo grinned. "Of course. But are you going to see Harry or Andre?"

"Both," Bobbi replied, grinning back. "But for different reasons," she hastily clarified.

◇

In the end they got their mother some Scottish tea and some Tunnock's tea cakes. They found their father a quaich, a small, traditional drinking bowl often made of pewter, silver or wood. The one they chose had a glass bottom on it, which the shop assistant told them was to ensure the user could keep an eye on their drinking companions as they sipped. They figured Dad would get a kick out of that.

◇

Once they were back in the cab, Connor suggested a water-front cafe for lunch where his niece Finella worked as maître d'. He parked outside and offered to pick them up in an hour, but Bobbi suggested he join them as their way of thanking him for his patience. He seemed rather chuffed that they'd asked.

The restaurant was surprisingly sleek and modern, at odds with the quaint surroundings. It was all glass and chrome, with white lilies and tablecloths and abstract art. Bobbi felt rather underdressed.

The woman who greeted them did not look at all like her uncle. Finella was tall and slim, perfectly groomed with sleek blonde hair and burgundy lipstick, but she gave Connor a warm hug and seemed pleased to see him.

"Fin, love, I'd like you to meet some friends of Kelly's. This here is Bobbi and her sister Jo, from New Zealand. They've been staying with him for a wee while, while they sort out some family matters."

Bobbi smiled and held out her hand. Finella offered the briefest touch of her fingers and a cool smile, before turning to retrieve menus and then indicating a table by the window. Pouring them each a glass of water, she looked at the sisters curiously.

"So, how on earth do you know Kelly? I had no idea he even knew anyone from New Zealand."

"Oh, we met him through Adam. And Kelly has been so wonderful, showing us around and cooking for us. He even took a day off to take us up to the priory to scatter our uncle's ashes," Jo told her.

"Bit of a disaster that turned out to be," Bobbi added. "I spent the whole night in the police station, while Jo and Kelly at least got stuck at an inn to wait out the storm."

Jo sputtered on her water and Bobbi turned to her. "You look flushed. Do you need the window open?"

"No, no, I'm fine."

Finella eyed Jo oddly. "Do you know what you'd like to drink, or do you need some more time?"

"Maybe a Pinot Gris, I think? Shall we share a bottle, Jo?"

"The usual for me, thanks, love," Connor told his niece before turning to Bobbi. "They stock Kelly's whisky here thanks to Finella."

"Oh, well. I might have one of those instead. I haven't tried it yet."

"Let's all have whisky," Jo agreed. "It's lovely."

"Kelly took Jo for a tour around the distillery," Bobbi told Connor.

Finella sniffed. "Did he now?"

There was an awkward pause. "I'll be right back with those drinks then."

They spent a few minutes looking over the menu and when Finella came back with the whisky, they all ordered the crab bisque that Connor recommended.

"So did you ladies get all your shopping done?"

Jo reached down to the shopping bags beside her and started to pull items out to show Connor, as though he'd never seen tea cakes or Scottish tea before.

She was carefully rewrapping the quaich when Finella returned with the food.

"You'll need to remove those if you want me to put these hot plates down," she said abruptly, and Jo hastily put everything back into the bag.

"Well, that smells delicious," Bobbi said politely, surprised at how cold Finella seemed to be towards them compared to how warmly she'd greeted her uncle when they'd arrived.

The food was lovely and Connor encouraged them to have a couple more whiskies, insisting he was in no rush to get back.

They sat and enjoyed their drinks. The sun was out, the water was sparkling blue and the air smelt fresh and cleansing as it does after a storm.

After Jo paid the bill, Finella helped carry the shopping to the car and gave Connor a hug. "I'll pop up and see you and Mary for lunch on my day off."

"That would be braw, she'd love to see you."

"Nice to meet you, Finella," Jo called to her retreating back.

◇

Connor drove the scenic route back. The road hugging the craggy coastline.

"What a fantastic place to live," Jo sighed contentedly from the front seat of the cab.

Connor agreed. Bobbi didn't answer. She was snoozing, mouth open, head lolling on her neck, snoring already.

CHAPTER 33

Jo

Bobbi made a pot of tea and she and Jo sat in Kelly's sheltered little garden enjoying the murky spring sunshine, or what there was of it. It wasn't particularly warm so they were wearing coats but the garden was pretty with pots of daffodils and crocuses and neatly trimmed bushes against the red-orange of the brick wall at the back. Marcus had never cared much for flowers, and their garden was mainly riverstone and grasses. Not very inspiring. They sat on red-painted wooden chairs, a lovely splash of extra colour. It was very peaceful.

Jo had baked cookies earlier and she nibbled one of the few that were left. Adam had managed to scoff most of them and was now in the kitchen making 'his signature dish', which Jo thought smelt like spaghetti bolognese. He said the key was to cook it for several hours. Earlier, he had shown her an album of photos of Hannah and himself when they were younger — both cute kids — and his mother, who looked like someone Jo would have liked, as well as a younger Kelly. The resemblance between Kelly and Adam was even more noticeable. Jo could also see his mother in him, whereas she thought Hannah looked like Kelly. There was a photo of the two of them dressed for what looked like her school ball. Kelly looked very proud.

They sat outside until it started to rain and then Bobbi went to lie down to read a new book she'd bought earlier and pack away their purchases from the day.

When she heard Kelly's car in the driveway, Jo felt a weird fluttering in her chest. She realised she'd been listening out for him, excited to see him again.

"Smells good," he called out, as he shucked off his coat in the hallway. He came into the room, his hair wet from the rain, reminding Jo of the night they had spent at the inn. She thought they might get a few minutes alone until Bobbi emerged from the bedroom.

"Jo, where did you put the tea cakes?"

"What do you mean? They're in the bag with the other stuff."

"Well, they're not. Are you sure you didn't leave them at the shop?"

"I definitely had them at the restaurant. Remember I took everything out to show Connor?"

"Well, maybe you left them there?"

"I'm pretty sure you can buy them at the store in town,"

Kelly told them.

Adam appeared in the living room, tea towel slung over his shoulder. "It's ready. Come and eat." There was an easiness about him since he'd spoken to his dad, Jo thought.

She and Bobbi insisted on clearing up afterwards and when they went back into the living room, Adam was setting up a game of Scrabble. Jo loved Scrabble. She was normally pretty mild-mannered but could get a little competitive when it came to games.

"Da," Adam protested after a while. Jo had just scored a decent thirty-six points by squeezing the word SQUAT onto the end of another word and covering a double-word tile. Then Kelly had his turn and put down SHAG.

"I don't think you can put rude words."

"Where's your mind at, son, it's the bird I'm referring to. What were you thinking?"

Adam flushed. "Aye, maybe, but you also put ROOT last time."

"The plant. Yer bum's oot the windae. I think maybe your mind's a bit much on this Thomas lad," Kelly teased, sneaking a sideways glance at Jo who was very intently studying her tiles.

He'd also put FIT and HOT earlier. She wasn't sure whether there was any significance or he just wasn't particularly good at Scrabble, even though he'd kind of chuckled when he'd placed the tiles on the board. Nobody else seemed to notice though.

She almost choked on her tea when on his next turn he started to put down JO but thankfully finished it off with UST.

Jo won and they celebrated with a bar of chocolate. The rain got heavier and lashed against the window. There was the distant rumble of thunder.

They'd just packed up the game when there was a sudden loud pounding on the door making them all jump. Jo wondered who it could be at this time of the night.

"I'll get it," Adam said.

It was James, Joan's husband. There had been an accident just down the road.

"Can you bring your truck, Kelly? There's a tree branch come down and it's over a car."

"Someone's trapped?" Kelly asked as he put his coat on and grabbed his keys.

"Aye, it's old Alan Leary, but if we can get the tree off, he'll get out easy enough. He's all right, not injured. It happened on the bend though and it'd be best to clear the road before anyone else comes round it, I'd say. The street lights are out as well, we need to act quick."

Kelly disappeared into the storm, leaving the three of them to drift off to bed.

◇

Bobbi fell asleep quickly, as she usually did, but Jo found herself lying awake, worrying about Kelly. Her ears strained to hear any unusual noises over the sound of Bobbi's snoring. Perhaps a car, veering around the bend and hitting the vehicle stuck in the middle of the road. Or, worse still, hitting Kelly as he tried to free the old man. Was that the wailing siren of an ambulance? It was most likely just the wind. Or perhaps the fire brigade arriving to help. She didn't know why she felt so anxious but was aware of her relief when she finally heard the front door open and then gently click shut, what seemed like hours afterwards.

She was thirsty anyway, she told herself, slipping quietly out of the room and shutting the door behind her. The house was warm from the central heating and she padded out to the kitchen, not bothering with a robe.

Kelly was there, his pale face reflecting in the moonlight that shone dimly through the window.

"Jo," he started as he turned towards her. "Did I wake you?"

"No, I couldn't sleep. I was worrying about you out in the storm." She noticed then that there was a large gash on Kelly's forehead. Blood trickled down towards his ear.

"Your head," she cried, moving towards him. "What happened?"

Kelly put his hand up to his face, gingerly feeling the cut.

"I almost got hit by the power lines as they fell," he told her.

Jo gasped. "Oh, my God, Kelly."

Kelly chuckled, looking a bit embarrassed. "I jumped out

of the way and slipped, must have done this when I hit my head on the car door. Silly bugger that I am."

"You could have been killed!" Jo felt stricken. "Sit down," she ordered, pushing him onto one of the stools at the breakfast bar. She ripped a cleaning cloth from the roll under the kitchen sink and wet it under the faucet.

"Is Mr Leary all right?"

"Aye, he's fine. A bit shook up but James was going to take him back to their place for the night. They'll have him checked out in the morning."

Jo gently took Kelly's face in one hand and dabbed the cloth carefully over the cut. It wasn't as deep as she'd first thought and didn't look like it needed stitching.

Kelly winced.

"Sorry." She pushed a stray lock of hair back from his face and continued to gently wash the blood away. "Do you have butterfly stitches or some plasters or something?"

"Aye, top cupboard above the sink. Adam was always injuring himself one way or another. It's still well stocked, I think."

Jo felt his eyes follow her as she moved to the cupboard and reached up for the first-aid kit. She suddenly wished she was wearing something other than an oversized I HEART SCOTLAND T-shirt and distinctly unsexy fluffy socks.

"Does it hurt much?" She fixed a large sticking plaster over her handiwork.

"It doesn't now," Kelly replied, eyeing her softly. "To be

honest with you, it's quite nice to have someone fussing over me and worrying about me again."

He reached up and took her hand, which was still lingering on his face, and then stood, pulling her towards him.

"Jo." He said her name softly.

He bent and kissed her before deftly lifting her to sit on the breakfast bar. His hands cupped the back of her head, fingers burrowing into her hair as they continued kissing. Jo slipped her hands under his T-shirt and over the still chilled skin of his back, sliding them up, feeling the firm muscles of his shoulders. Next thing she knew, her legs were straddling Kelly, her knickers somehow discarded on the kitchen floor. She wanted this moment to last forever, she thought.

After that, she stopped thinking altogether.

◇

Later, Jo and Kelly crept down the hallway, stopping at Jo's door, giggling like teenagers. Kelly kissed her goodnight for quite a while before she snuck back into her room. It was like standing outside your parents' house, hoping they wouldn't still be awake and nobody was peering out the window. Thankfully, Bobbi was still dead to the world and, as a bonus, had turned over, and although still breathing deeply, had stopped snoring.

It was still some time before Jo was able to fall asleep. She was sure she had a huge, sappy grin on her face.

◇

The following morning, Jo put on a robe and went into the kitchen where she found Bobbi sitting at the breakfast bar with a cup of tea.

"There's porridge on the stove if you want some. And tea in the pot."

Jo mumbled her thanks and took a bowl from the cupboard, avoiding looking Bobbi in the eye. She was pretty sure neither she nor Kelly had been thinking clearly enough to wipe down the breakfast bar the night before. She wasn't going to think about it, she decided.

"Kelly gone into work?" she asked Bobbi casually.

"No idea. His car was gone when I got up, so I guess so. I've got a bit of work to do myself this morning. How about you?"

"I thought I might do a bit of washing and pack up my stuff." She gazed pensively out the window, glad Bobbi couldn't see her expression. They had planned to head back to London the next day and she knew Bobbi was looking forward to it. She'd been talking about things she wanted to do there. Normally Jo would have been equally enthusiastic but she wasn't so keen to be leaving now. Would it be crazy to stay longer?

Within less than a minute of each other, both her and Bobbi's phones dinged with texts. Doreen.

What are you two up to? I was so embarrassed when everyone thought Bayley had died! I had so many phone calls. What are you playing at?

They looked at each other and, by unspoken agreement, both hit delete.

◇

"I thought you ladies might like to take a walk out to the lighthouse with me this afternoon."

Kelly arrived home just before lunch. Jo said it sounded like a great idea.

"I think I'll pass," Bobbi replied. "I haven't got any decent walking shoes with me and I need to get some washing done and packed up for tomorrow too."

"Oh aye, you should do that," Kelly replied.

Adam was standing staring into the open refrigerator as though new food would magically appear there.

"I might come out for a walk."

"You should probably crack on with some of that schoolwork you've missed, lad, especially if you're wanting to go down to London next week to see that Harry fella."

So he and Jo put on jackets and walking shoes and, although it wouldn't have been far to walk, drove up to the base of the track. There were a couple of cars parked outside the cafe but there didn't seem to be any people about. The lighthouse had been automated since 1993, Kelly told her as they walked. He could remember when they'd had lighthouse keepers out there and it had always been a favourite spot of his to come.

"The lighthouse was built by the Stevenson brothers. One

of them was the father of Robert Louis Stevenson who wrote *Treasure Island*. I always think of that when I'm out here."

What a charming image, Jo thought as she snuck a sideways look at Kelly. He was looking particularly handsome in a green corduroy jacket with a checked lining. His scarf wrapped snugly around his neck.

It was a lovely day with a light wind. Jo couldn't have thought of a more romantic setting as they hiked through the reserve along the rock cliffs.

"Did your wife — Linda, isn't it? Did she like to walk?"

"Nae, she wasn't much of a walker. Beautiful piano player and could sing like an angel though. Must be where Adam gets it from. I sound like a strangled donkey."

"And she was from around here as well?"

"Linda was from near Birmingham, which is why I think Hannah chose to go there for university. She tolerated living out here but she never really loved it like I do. When she had the accident five years ago she was coming back from visiting her sister in London." He stared out to the horizon as he spoke. "How about you, Jo? Was your ex a walker?"

"No. In fact we didn't have much at all in common really. Marcus and I grew to be very different people in the end. I guess we stayed together because of Bayley. It was silly really, she never needed for us to stay together. I put up with a lot of stuff, even the first time he cheated, but that just made me a fool because he did it again. I'd never be that stupid now." She took off her woollen gloves and stuffed them into the pocket of her jacket. "Anyway, Marcus wasn't a walker, but I love to get out and experience nature. He's more of a couch potato. He never did anything he didn't want to do. Actually, he wasn't one for romantic gestures at all; I can't think of a single time he did anything memorable."

Jo realised she was rambling. "Sorry, you probably didn't need to hear all that," she said sheepishly.

Kelly shook his head. "Sounds like you're well rid of him."

"Yes, I'm ready to move on now. Time to find myself."

"You deserve to be happy," Kelly said gruffly.

She stopped and breathed in the fresh air, staring out to sea where the water sparkled invitingly.

"Kelly, this is just stunning." She pointed to a bird, circling near the cliff, and gave him a cheeky smirk. "Is that a shag?"

Kelly laughed loudly. "That's a guillemot. It's breeding season right now. Must be something in the air," he grinned widely. "Now that over there; *that's* a shag."

The lighthouse itself wasn't open to the public but they had a wander around past the whitewashed keep buildings and then down to the lighthouse, which wasn't large but set in a beautiful location. They walked down the path to the rocky outcrop where the foghorn was situated.

"When I was a young lad the foghorn signal could be heard in the village, but they dinnae use it now," Kelly said sadly. They trudged back up the steps and started walking back. Jo wasn't sure when but at some point he'd taken her hand.

When they arrived back at the car Kelly opened the back

door and with a flourish pulled out a picnic basket and the rug that Jo had used to try to keep warm when they were at the priory. There were a few muddy marks on it but Kelly spread it out on the sheltered side behind the car and started to produce an assortment of things from the basket. There was a thermos of hot coffee, ham and chutney sandwiches, squidgy chocolate brownie and some crisp apples that he must have picked up on his way home.

When they'd eaten and packed everything away again, they lay on the rug staring up at the sky, not saying much. Kelly took her hand again and absently rubbed her thumb with his own. Jo was feeling pleasantly sleepy. She could stay there all day. They rolled to face each other and Kelly reached over and brushed the hair back off her face, before leaning in and giving her a long kiss.

"I dinnae why but I feel like a horny teenager when I'm around you."

Jo pulled him closer and threw her leg over his as they both eagerly resumed kissing.

Kelly had just unzipped her coat and was working on the buttons of her shirt while Jo's hands had wandered down to Kelly's belt buckle, when they heard a noise, like someone clearing their throat.

"Ach, sorry, dinnae mean to disturb you two lovebirds. You just carry on with your shenanigans."

Jo looked up startled to see Connor towering above them. Kelly had rolled off her and she quickly zipped her jacket, hoping Connor hadn't got too much of an eyeful.

The taxi was parked over near the cafe. Connor took a drag of his cigarette. "Just brought a couple of visitors out to see the lighthouse," he continued, not really giving them a chance to carry on with their shenanigans after all. "I saw your car, Kelly, but I didnae realise you were hiding out back here." He grinned, then tapped the side of his nose and winked before turning and walking off, chuckling to himself.

Kelly sighed ruefully as they got up, folded the picnic rug and got back into the car.

CHAPTER 34

Bobbi

Bobbi had been lying on the bed, thinking about Andre. Wondering if he'd noticed her absence at the shows they'd missed. He probably wasn't expecting to see them again now, she reasoned.

She was hoping he'd missed her. She was going to make sure he saw her in London, she decided. Life was too short not to at least try to make your dreams come true. Or fantasies, she supposed in this case.

She was having a lovely little daydream and planning what to wear and say when she heard a voice call out from the foyer.

"Yoo-hoo. Anyone home?"

She headed up the hallway and found Joan from the pub. She'd come in and was putting a basket, covered in a checked tea towel, on the dining room table.

"Och, hello, pet," she called when she spotted Bobbi. "I baked some scones. We never did get a chance to say hello proper like the other day."

Bobbi smiled at the older woman in thanks.

"They smell lovely," she said, lifting one corner and peeping in. "Can I make you a tea? Coffee?"

"Och, now, a tea'd be lovely, but dinnae fash yourself, I know where things are, I'll get it."

Bobbi sat, a little dumbfounded, as Joan set about putting on the kettle, fetching mugs and plates and the milk from Kelly's fridge. She wasn't sure if this was common practice in small villages like St Abbs, although she wasn't complaining, as the older woman set a still-warm scone on her plate and proceeded to produce a small pot of jam and some butter from inside the basket too.

"'Twas lovely to see you two down at Mac's," she continued as she poured. "The gals and I love a bit of excitement and the village is all about you two right now, and your Uncle Bill's wee quest."

Bobbi wasn't sure what to say to that, but it didn't seem to matter as Joan kept up the chatter.

"We were hoping Kelly might fetch you all down tonight to join us for quiz night. I know Kelly's a dab hand at the tricky questions, being that he's so knowledgeable and all. I could sign you all up, no worries like, when I pop down later to fetch James? He's taken poor old Alan down for a pint after his wee scare last night."

Jo loved quiz nights, Bobbi thought. And they had nothing else planned for their last night in St Abbs, so she agreed, hoping Kelly and Adam would be up for it.

Joan was very forthcoming with the general 'knowledge' herself, Bobbi discovered when she proceeded to tell her all the gossip in the village. The local postman had taken two days off last week and they all thought perhaps he and the wife had split, and the bakery was having a sale, but they should avoid that as it meant they'd over-baked and were getting rid of the old stuff, warmed up again. Joan was enlightening.

Then she told Bobbi all about Kelly and his wife Linda, and how sad it had been when she'd been in the car accident. They all thought very highly of Kelly and they were pleased to see him out and about, and smiling.

"I imagine there aren't too many romantic prospects in the village for him."

"Nae, I suppose that's why he got back together with Finella last year. They were high school sweethearts, you know. Before Linda. Connor said you'd met Finella at lunch."

"We did." She was not sure what else to say. "The food was lovely. I didn't realise they were a couple."

"Aye. Anyway, tell me about yourself, Bobbi. Do you have a husband waiting at home for you?"

She managed to drag out more information about Bobbi and Jo than a detective could, and when she finally left, Bobbi felt a little drained. She made another cup of tea then helped herself to another scone. They really were delicious. And obviously fresher than she'd find at the local bakery, she reasoned.

◇

Kelly and Jo finally got back from their walk and Bobbi remarked that they looked very windblown and glowing from the sea air. Jo was quite pink, in fact.

Weirdly, they hadn't seemed overly keen about the quiz, which was odd. Jo had an almost photographic memory when it came to trivia and she'd thought she would be dead keen to show it off. Joan had also seemed adamant that Kelly would enjoy it.

After a few feeble attempts to get out of it, they finally agreed to go and Bobbi had wandered off to tell Adam he was required to be their fourth team member.

◇

The pub was packed and, according to Adam, every villager and his dog was there. It seemed there was some truth in that, Bobbi observed, when he stopped to pat a Border collie under a table on their way in.

Mac had very kindly put a reserved sign on a booth for them and Kelly and Jo had squeezed into the cushioned ledge against the window, while Bobbi offered to get the first round.

There was a sign-up sheet on the bar, as well as notepads

and pens to write down answers. They needed a team name, so Bobbi wrote 'Clan Kiwi' down and ordered them all drinks from a young girl working the bar.

Some of the punters from the other day came over to say hello, and there was a quick rundown for some of the eavesdroppers/bystanders explaining about their little quest for Uncle Bill. Bobbi was hoping the conversation wouldn't go round in a convoluted maze again, and was pleased for the distraction when she felt a tap on her leg. A minuscule, wizened woman peered up at Bobbi through her half-glasses and poked her again with an intricately carved walking stick. Wearing a long woollen dress, she had a large mole on her cheek and a moustache to rival Mac's.

"And what do we call you then?" she shouted up at Bobbi. Her voice was a lot louder than her size would suggest.

"I'm Bobbi," she replied with a kind smile. Dear old thing.

"Nae, I mean what are you," the woman boomed, "a lad or a lassie? Barney didnae say."

Bobbi wasn't sure what she was getting at, and must have looked a little confused. Was it the unisex name? She really disliked using her full name.

"It's just that we dinnae want to mess up the pronouns," a kindly middle-aged woman told her, patting her awkwardly on the arm. "We dinnae get many drag queens around here."

Bobbi was lost for words. She looked around. The entire pub seemed to have paused in mid-action and were speech-less, waiting for her reply. What the—? Oh, my God, she was going to throttle Barney.

"It's Roberta," she got out through gritted teeth. "I'm a female, and I'm *not* a drag queen, I just own a drag bar."

"What did you say?" the evil little midget asked, and Bobbi leant down and loudly said, "No penis, all vagina here, lady," in a most unladylike manner.

She took her pad and pen, and stormed back to the table, leaving Kelly to get up and fetch the drinks.

Connor had just come in and gave them a cheery wave. Bobbi noticed a deep flush spread over Jo's face. "Are you okay? You look hot. Take your scarf and beanie off," Bobbi said distractedly as she looked around for Barney. And a rusty knife to castrate him with.

Jo mumbled something, and unwound her scarf, looking around furtively. "You're acting very odd," Bobbi grumbled.

Adam came over carrying their drinks. Bobbi looked over to see what had happened to Kelly. He was surrounded by a group of the village fishermen, all guffawing, patting him on the back, shaking his hand and beaming. He looked very sheepish and kept glancing over at their table. Weird. She'd have to remember to ask him what that was all about.

Eventually he returned with even more drinks. Handy, because Jo had downed hers rather quickly and Bobbi always liked having a backup ready to go. Kelly mumbled something about Connor shouting them a round then choked out a laugh and looked down at his feet as though he were examining his boots for mud or something.

Adam told them he had been talking to Colleen and that she was going to let him sing there on Saturday night as a trial. Just covers, he said. Sort of like an open mic thing, he enthused.

They all cheers-ed to that and then Pete sent over another round on him. They'd all be blind drunk before the quiz even started at this rate. Perhaps that was the plan. The sneaky buggers.

Eileen wandered past, giving them a little wave, and then Mac was standing on a chair booming at them to all hush down so they could get started.

There were several teams and Mac announced that there would be twenty-five questions in total, with categories of sport, entertainment, general knowledge, science, and inventions.

Each round they would give the answers and tally points, he declared. There was to be no cheating, he added sternly, and outlined the rules briefly.

Jo and Kelly seemed to be taking it very seriously and kept reminding Bobbi and Adam not to call out any answers too loudly, for fear of the other teams hearing.

Adam and Bobbi rolled their eyes at each other and grinned. "Da, can I order some hot chips?" Adam asked, then wandered off to wait in the line to order.

Bobbi finally spotted one of the cops from the station the other night and was about to head over and make a scene when Mac dinged the bell to start round one.

They started with sports. Bobbi's knowledge here was sadly lacking, but they did okay, getting four out of five correct, including one 'educated' guess from Jo that she was thrilled to get right. Kelly was very impressed and kept saying so.

Mac read out each of the team's scores, and also some of the more amusing answers that had been submitted. "No, Joan," he said, "'ball scratching' is not the correct term for answer two."

There was a lot of ribbing, and fake arguments and laughter, and Bobbi was on drink five without leaving the table, when they started the second round. Inventions.

They scored 100% on that round, and there was raucous laughter at John's answer to the question 'What kitchen appliance did Percy Spencer invent to save time?'

Mac boomed loudly, "We were looking for a microwave there, John, not a wife."

Kelly knew that Shakespeare invented the word 'vomit', which Bobbi told Jo might be a useful fact for her to remember.

They announced a break then, and Bobbi joined the mad rush for the ladies. She was next up, when Mary emerged from the stall and gave her a cheery grin.

"Och, hen, I heard Kelly and your sister had a lovely romp up at our lighthouse this morn."

She smiled at Mary, and agreed that Jo had come back saying she'd had a ball.

There were muffled snorty sounds from the other stall.

She was busting to go by this stage, and didn't linger. She didn't want a repeat of the incident that had ruined her brand new Italian suede boots a few years back.

Back at the table, Adam's order had arrived. He'd gotten fish bites and crab sticks too, so they all dug in with relish, needing it to soak up some of the alcohol. Another round of drinks sat waiting, this one from Seamus, Jo told her before heading off to the bathroom herself.

She was back just in time for round three, and the entertainment questions.

Bobbi was thrilled when the first question was 'What was the name of the poison used in *The Princess Bride*?'

She leant over and told Kelly the answer. "Iocane," she said, beaming. Then thinking of Andre.

She and Jo had a great laugh at the question 'Who is Reginald Dwight better known as?' yelling out "Elton John" far too loudly, much to Kelly's disgust.

Kelly was the only one in their team who hadn't known the answer to 'Who co-wrote the TV show *Gavin & Stacey* with Ruth Jones?' Good old James Corden.

There were a variety of wrong answers from all the teams for the question 'What is Johnny Depp afraid of?' From Pete's 'pirates' to 'being sober' from Connor. No one got clowns.

Adam got the question right about the number of keys on a baby grand piano. They were the only ones, which put them in the lead by one point with Seamus's team close behind.

The science round was a bit dull for Bobbi, so she and

Adam played tic-tac-toe on bar napkins while Kelly and Jo had lots of whispered discussions over what to write down.

They came out tied with Seamus, and they were really the only two teams in the running. The prize was a bottle of bubbles and a meat pack donated by Smith's butchers, so Bobbi wasn't too concerned about winning, but Jo had that competitive glint in her eye, and Kelly was now covering the answers as he wrote them down in case of spies and sabotage.

What a pair, thought Bobbi with a grin as she sipped her gin.

The final round started, and the pub was getting rowdier, more rambunctious. The revelry increased tenfold when the answer was 'laughter' to the question 'What does the average person do thirteen times a day?' Bobbi decided these people were far from average.

At the end of the round they were tied with Seamus and tensions were high when Mac announced there would be a tie-breaker. It was like a gift from God when the question was 'What is New Zealand's biggest export industry?'

Jo clapped excitedly and leant over to whisper the answer in Kelly's ear. He looked a little dubious and asked "Are you sure?" Jo insisted, and he reluctantly wrote it down. They handed their answer sheet in to Mac and sat back to await the results.

Mac called out the final answer and Jo looked thrilled. Seamus had wrongly guessed farming, so it seemed that they had won, until Mac started to laugh uproariously. "I dinnae think *terrorism* is that big in New Zealand, Kelly."

Jo was staring at Kelly with an incredulous look on her face. "Terrorism?" she seethed.

"Aye. That's what you told me," Kelly said defensively.

"*Tourism.* I said tourism!" Jo shouted.

"Well, I couldnae understand your accent," Kelly shouted back. They glared at each other for a few seconds before they both started laughing. Jo and Bobbi were still cackling when they got home and climbed into bed.

Bobbi was exhausted: she'd drunk far too much and it was late, but she'd had a surprisingly good night in the end. Drag queen incident aside. It was a great way to end their visit to St Abbs, she thought as she lay in bed, hoping to dream of Andre and not rodents of unusual size.

CHAPTER 35

Jo

It had turned out to be a great night out.

When Jo and Kelly arrived back from their walk, Bobbi told them about Joan's visit and how she'd entered them as a team for the pub quiz that night. She and Kelly exchanged a quick glance, both thinking about Connor and wondering whether by now the whole village would know that their local whisky maker had been getting his end away in a very public place.

But Jo did love a quiz, so she put her misgivings aside. They could have won too, Jo speculated, if Kelly hadn't misheard her final answer. She'd grumbled about it for the rest of the evening, Kelly feebly tried to defend himself, and Bobbi and Adam had rolled their eyes.

Now she was lying in bed, thinking of Kelly. They were packed and ready to leave for London the next day. Kelly had offered to drive them into Berwick-upon-Tweed to catch the train and, as much as she was looking forward to seeing Harry in concert again, she really didn't want to leave. She thought about how Kelly had kissed her that afternoon and the look in his eyes just before he did. She felt elated, she realised, like she was floating. It had been a long time since she'd felt that way; she couldn't even remember it. Bobbi was sleeping, breathing deeply and evenly. Careful not to make any noise that might wake her, Jo slipped out of bed and down the hallway to Kelly's room, where she knocked softly before opening the door. She was just going to apologise for being so competitive, she told herself. Nothing more.

◇

One fantastic shag later, they lay facing each other in the bed, Jo's pulse still racing. Kelly lifted her hand and kissed her palm. "I know it's only been a week and this sounds crazy, but I feel like there could be something real between us. I don't want you to go."

"I feel the same way," Jo said softly.

"Would you think about coming back after London?"

"I'd really like that."

◇

As she closed Kelly's door gently behind her quite some time later, she was startled by a noise. Adam. Exactly what she had been trying to avoid by going discreetly back to her room, but to her surprise he just gave a little chuckle and a thumbs up as he passed her in the hallway. He didn't seem at all shocked.

Jo slipped back into bed, grateful that Bobbi was still asleep and oblivious. There was no way she could sleep. It was like her head was about to combust, thoughts of what the future might hold spinning about like a whirling dervish.

CHAPTER 36

Bobbi

The next morning as Bobbi was taking their bags to the car, she opened the door to find Finella there, about to knock, a packet of Tunnock's tea cakes in her hand.

"Oh, hello, Debbie," she said, as she pushed past Bobbi into the house.

"It's Bobbi," Bobbi muttered, trailing behind her into the kitchen where Kelly and Jo sat having a cup of tea.

"Hello, Kel darling." Finella bent and kissed Kelly on the cheek, placing the tea cakes onto the table. "Your guests left these at the restaurant. Looks like I'm just in time, are they off?"

"Hello, Finella, that's very kind of you, but we managed to find some in the village," Jo told her.

Kelly seemed a little flustered. "I hadn't realised you'd met. We're just about to head to the station actually."

Bobbi reached over and opened the packet. "We could try these ones now with our cup of tea. Can I make you something?"

"No, I won't stay, but I'll probably see you for a drink at Mac's later, Kel."

Bobbi shrugged, took a tea cake and passed the box to Jo, who shook her head.

"Right, well, safe trip home, ladies. Kel, if you're driving all that way, I suppose you're going to stop in and see Bob and Nyree?"

"Aye, I'm planning on dropping Adam there."

"Well, give them my love."

"Will do. Let me walk you out."

Finella gave a small smile as she followed Kelly to the front door.

Jo looked puzzled. "Well, that was weird. Fancy coming all this way just to return a box of biscuits. Especially since she doesn't seem to like us much. Anyone would think she wanted to get into Kelly's pants."

Bobbi snorted. "I'd say she's been there plenty of times."

"What do you mean?"

"Well, she is his girlfriend."

"What? No she's not."

"She is. Joan told me. Apparently they went out in high school and they got back together again after Kelly's wife died."

Why did Jo look so shocked? She stood, pushing her seat

back from the table and turned to rinse her cup at the sink.

"I'll just have a final check of the room," she said in a quiet voice, leaving without looking at Bobbi.

Bobbi ate another tea cake. Then stuck another one in her pocket for later.

Kelly came back in and picked up the bags.

"Adam," he called, "if you're coming with us we need to leave right now."

Adam came thundering down the stairs but Bobbi beat him out the door.

"Shotgun!" she called, giving him a grin.

Bobbi and Adam argued over the music selection while they waited for Jo.

"Should I go in and get her?" Kelly asked, checking his watch.

Jo appeared then, wearing sunglasses. She hopped into the back seat with Adam.

"Did you text Gran to remind them you're coming?" Kelly asked, starting the car and pulling out onto the road.

"Yes, Da," Adam sighed.

◇

The car trip was uneventful, although Jo was a little quiet, Bobbi noticed. She was probably just tired, perhaps missing Bayley. She might suggest they FaceTime again tonight since she wanted to check in with Sam about the wages and a couple of work emails she'd received.

It seemed like he had everything under control though, and Bobbi was grateful she had him. He probably deserved a raise. It was funny to think of Bayley and Sam back home, all loved up in her apartment. She checked the time and tried to calculate what time it would be there now. She could never work it out with daylight saving and different time zones. Jo would know though.

She and Adam talked a little about the London concert and Bobbi reiterated her invite to come and see her in Wellington. She joked with Adam that he could sing at her bar if he was willing to put on a dress.

"Well, if Harry can do it," he laughed.

◇

The station was crowded and, as usual, Bobbi was in need of a pee, so she offered to sort out the tickets while Jo and Kelly unloaded their bags. She'd meet Jo at the ticket booth.

She hugged Kelly and Adam goodbye, promising to stay in touch and thanking them again for their wonderful hospitality.

They had planned to be heading back from the Glasgow station on an earlier train, so she had to credit those tickets and have new ones issued. The ticketing agent was not pleased. She was a plump, middle-aged woman wearing a knit jumper with a horse on it. Her face matched.

It was Saturday morning and she seemed like she didn't love her job, Bobbi noted as she sighed her way through the process, tapping away at the computer. She finally handed over two new tickets with a very monotone "Enjoy your trip."

◇

They hadn't managed to get a table this time and Jo was sitting looking out the window as the train bumped along. She made very quiet 'yes' and 'no' replies to all the things Bobbi asked her.

Bobbi had gone to the food carriage for some sandwiches and watery takeaway cups of tea but Jo hadn't even sipped hers. She watched out of the corner of her eye as Jo rubbed her sleeve across her face. Was she crying?

"Jo? Are you okay?" she questioned gently.

Jo wiped her eyes again and did a little shuddery sigh. "Shit. I'm being ridiculous. Sorry."

"What's going on?" Bobbi queried. "Missing Bayley?"

"No, it's Kelly," Jo said quietly.

"Kelly? What about Kelly?"

"I've got all emotionally attached," Jo said, her voice hitching.

Bobbi was a bit lost. She felt like she was missing something.

"What do you mean? Is there some reason — I mean, he's a really nice guy but what gave you the idea — wait. Did you and Kelly hook up?"

Jo nodded.

"What the hell? When?" Bobbi was incredulous. How had

she not picked up on this?

"Well, the first time was the night of the storm."

"The first time? How many times did you bonk?" Bobbi's voice was getting louder and Jo shushed her, blushing as she looked around to see who had heard.

"How many times have you shagged?" Bobbi demanded.

"A few," was Jo's embarrassed answer, "but I didn't know he had a bloody girlfriend."

Wow. Bobbi tried to focus on the fact that Jo was upset, not on the fact that her sister hadn't told her about this major event in her life. She thought they told each other everything.

Jo did a sad little sob and fumbled in her bag for a tissue.

"It's bad enough to be cheated on but now he's made me into the other woman. He still had the cheek at the station to ask me if I'd come back."

"What did you say?"

"I said no, and then I just left. I didn't even wait to see what lame excuse he'd come up with."

Shit. Bobbi didn't know what to say. She'd never seen Jo like this.

"Well, good for you. Want me to kill him for you?"

Jo attempted a laugh.

They were silent for a bit. "Wait," Bobbi accused, "so, were you shagging while I was in the clink?"

"Ah, yeah," Jo said, and her lips twitched a little.

"Hmmm. So how was it?" Bobbi asked with a grin.

"Well, let's just say, I didn't realise how badly Marcus was lacking in the bagpipe department until now." They both laughed and sat in comfortable silence.

"Did you know," Jo said, "that hyenas shag six times a day? Probably explains why they're so happy."

Bobbi snorted. "I love you, Jo," she said.

Jo leant her head on Bobbi's shoulder and sighed deeply. "Love you too, Bob."

She really did sound miserable.

◇

When they arrived in London, the station was hectic. They had to push and shove to grab their bags, and make their way through the crowd to try to get a taxi. They were staying in Kings Cross in a nice boutique hotel. They'd decided to splurge a little on the accommodation since they'd saved a fair bit of their budget staying at Kelly's.

The reception was thankfully quiet after what had felt like a long and rather emotional train trip and they got checked into their room quickly. It was lovely and roomy, with two big twin beds, and a bath as well as a shower.

Jo's phone rang.

"Shit, it's him again."

"Give it to me. I'll talk to him." She grabbed the phone from Jo and hit 'Accept' launching into her rant.

"Listen, you cheating aresehole. Jo is not interested in being your other woman. She's had enough of scummy men who think they can have their cake and eat it too. You and

Finella can fuck right off." She turned the phone off and gave it back to Jo who flopped down on the closest bed and lay looking at the ceiling.

Perhaps they need a drink? There was a directory on the coffee table with general information, so Bobbi flipped through it looking for the mini-bar prices to see how astronomical they were. They were. Very.

"Ohh, there's an indoor pool, spa and sauna," she informed Jo. "We could go for a soak?"

"Maybe," Jo replied, not sounding very enthusiastic. She got up and hefted her suitcase onto the bed and unzipped it. Then she shrieked and slammed it closed before leaping back and falling over Bobbi onto her bed.

"Ow. What the hell, Jo?"

"Holy cheesus!" Jo shrieked again "I think there's a body in there."

Bobbi was confused. "In where? Your suitcase?"

"Yeah — I don't think that's my suitcase," said Jo in a shaky voice.

They both eyed said suitcase warily. After a minute, Bobbi said, "A dead body?"

"Well, would a live body be sitting quietly in a medium-sized suitcase waiting for us to invite them out?" Jo replied tartly.

"All right, all right, no need to be snarky," Bobbi grumbled. "Open it again then and have another look."

Jo looked pleadingly at her sister, doing her sad eyes.

"Can you?"

Bobbi gulped. "Do you think we should call the reception? Or the cops? Was there blood?"

Jo shook her head. "I don't think so, but I didn't get a good look. I just saw a face."

Bobbi leant over towards the suitcase. She listened intently for a bit, and then sniffed at it suspiciously. Then she gingerly lifted the bag tag. "Gerald Parker," she read out.

"Yep, not your bag," she confirmed rather unnecessarily. "This is why I have a very visibly striking bag, you know, and not a plain black one. Otherwise, they all look the same."

Jo looked at Bobbi's Hello Kitty-inspired case in hot pink.

"Right, thanks for that," she said drily. "I'll remember that next time I mix up my case with that of a serial killer." They contemplated the suitcase again.

"If there's a dead body in there, I think we should call the cops," Bobbi declared, "but you've already put your fingerprints on it, so I think we should check to be sure." She nudged Jo and inclined her head towards the case.

Jo took a deep breath, then another, and then reached over, eyes squeezed shut, to quickly flip the suitcase lid open. They both cautiously peeked in.

There was definitely a body folded up in there. It wasn't alive. It also wasn't dead. Her silicon lips were open in a pouty-lipped 'O'. Her large bosom and pert nipples stood out from the lacy bustier she wore. Next to her was a half-used tube of lube.

"Oh. My. God," Jo said, her hand over her mouth.

"Ewwwww," said Bobbi at the same time.

The fancy-looking sex doll stared back at them with realistic but glassy eyes and said nothing.

"Fuck me. What a crapper of a day," said Jo.

"That's what she said," Bobbi joked. "Still, at least we didn't make total dicks of ourselves by calling the cops," she added, trying to look on the bright side.

Jo spent a painful twenty minutes pushing buttons on the automated line for National Rail before discovering there was now no one at the lost and found department. They'd have to try again in the morning.

They weren't quite sure what to do with 'Mona', as they'd named her. Eventually they zipped her back up, shoved the case into the coat cupboard next to the ironing board, and tried not to think about her.

It was getting late, so they decided it would be easier to order room service than go out. Jo borrowed a T-shirt and they settled in to watch an in-house movie while they ate their chicken Caesar salads and New York baked cheesecakes.

"Poor Gerald, he might not be able to sleep tonight without Mona," Bobbi said as she made them both a chamomile tea.

"I just hope she doesn't snore too," was Jo's sarcastic reply.

◇

They were both fast asleep when the phone rang. Jo sat bolt upright and shouted "Shit — someone's dead!" which caused

Bobbi to attempt to fling herself out of the bed, with limited success. Her feet tangled in the sheets and she ended up falling head first onto the carpet, while Jo fumbled around trying to find the switch for the bedside light.

Eventually, Bobbi found her phone and looked at the screen.

"Bloody hell," she groaned, "it's Doreen."

She hit 'Answer' and put it on speaker before saying, "Mum? Everything okay?"

"Hi, love," her mother's voice said loudly. "Am I talking on your smartie phone? Can you hear me okay?"

Bobbi and Jo rolled their eyes at each other.

"You don't need to shout, Mum," said Jo irritably.

"Oh, hello, is that you, Jo?" Doreen went on. "I thought I'd rung your sister."

"You did, Mum," said Jo patiently. "You're just on speaker."

"Oh, good, good. Well, I'm worried about your father," Doreen continued. "He's been on the loo all afternoon. I told him I should take him to see Doctor Sheldon but I'm worried about my car seats."

Bobbi and Jo shared another pained and confused look.

"What about your car seats?" Jo asked.

"What? Oh, well, I just had them valeted and if he has an accident—"

"Jesus H Christ," Bobbi muttered. "Mum, you do realise it's three in the morning here, right?"

"Hmmmm? Oh, it's not here," Doreen said, sounding completely unfazed. "It's about two-thirty, I think. I have the mahjong ladies coming at four. What if your father is still in the bathroom? I need to get in there and air it out. I'd be mortified if—"

"Mum," Jo said, a little sharper than usual. "What would you like us to do?"

There was a small silence, and then Doreen said a little huffily, "Well, I just wanted your advice in case your father was deathly ill. But if you don't care ..."

Bobbi and Jo waited, but she had trailed off. This was obviously the part where they were supposed to say 'Of course we care, Mum,' etc. etc. The silence stretched until Bobbi said, "What do you think is wrong with Dad then?" and Doreen was off again.

"Well, he seems to think it was the Ritchies," she said in a hushed tone, as if said neighbours three doors down might hear her.

"We had dinner at theirs last night. It was curry. Quite spicy. I had to take a pill when I got home. So I'm worried it's food poisoning. But your father says he's just got a touch of Delhi belly. Can you get that in New Zealand?"

Bobbi groaned. "I'm sure he's fine, Mum, I wouldn't worry."

"I think you just have to let it run its course, Mum," said Jo, trying to sound sympathetic. Bobbi mouthed 'run its course' and silently laughed beside her.

In the background, they heard their father's voice calling out and then Doreen announced, "I have to go, girls, your father needs some more toilet paper. Ring me later. Oh, but not till the evening, or even tomorrow, but after lunch, because I have the village committee meeting and I have to make club sandwiches. I'm coming — hold your horses," she shouted, presumably at their father, and then she hung up.

Bobbi put the phone back down on the bedside table, while Jo sorted her sheets. They got back into bed and Jo flicked off the lamp.

They both lay in the dark.

"But enough about me, how are you two? Having a good time on your holiday?" Jo muttered.

Bobbi laughed. "At least she didn't ask if we'd been behaving ourselves."

CHAPTER 37

Jo

Mona was, thankfully, a quiet sleeper, but Jo had a problem the next day because she had no luggage and wasn't prepared to wear the red satin maid's outfit or whatever it was — she didn't want to look too closely — that scantily covered Mona. She borrowed a pair of jeans from Bobbi, as well as a canary-yellow top that she really didn't think suited her complexion. After a quick breakfast at the hotel they headed back to the station to see if Gerald Parker had turned Jo's bag in.

"She's not going to bite, Jo," Bobbi said, noticing that Jo was holding Mona in her almost-identical-to-Jo's black bag at a strange angle away from her body.

But Jo countered that they had no idea where Mona, or the bag, had been and it was better to be safe than sorry.

The station was busy and a chirpy attendant pointed them in the direction of lost property. They waited while an elderly man had his umbrella returned to him and then approached the counter, Jo lugging the suitcase with her.

"I seem to have mixed my bag up with another passenger on the train yesterday," she told the attendant, who had a crooked staff name tag announcing he was 'Steven'.

"I was hoping someone may have handed mine in. This bag here belongs to Gerald Parker."

"'Ow do you know it belongs to Gerald Parker?" Steven asked, peering suspiciously at her through his thick glasses.

"Because," Jo said pleasantly, "there is a name tag stating that it belongs to Gerald Parker."

"Maybe someone swapped the tags over. Did you think of that?"

"I didn't, but the contents of the bag most definitely don't belong to me."

"So you opened someone else's bag, even though it didn't belong to you?"

"Well, I wasn't aware it wasn't my bag until I opened it," Jo told him patiently.

"Even when it had a name tag saying 'Gerald Parker'?"

"Look, Steven," Bobbi interjected with a deep sigh. She hefted the bag onto the counter, unzipped it and flipped open the lid.

"This doesn't belong to us and we would like to return her to her rightful owner. These dolls can be very expensive. I imagine her owner is pretty eager to get her back."

Steven was bug-eyed behind his glasses.

"That's disgusting," he squeaked, when he regained some of his composure. "We can't have that kind of thing in here. It's not even hygienic." He took a step back from the counter, looking at them in horror.

Two older ladies had entered the room while they were talking and both perked up their ears, coming closer to see what the offending object might be.

"I've never seen one of them before," one lady said, peering between Jo and Bobbi to get a better look. "Well, it takes all sorts, doesn't it? Nothing to be offended about, young man."

Steven huffed and indicated to Bobbi that she should zip the bag back up. He then jotted down some details in a large notebook and went off to see whether Jo's bag had been handed in the day before. It had. She was thankful to make the swap and they made their way out of the station.

As they exited, Bobbi nudged Jo. "Do you think any of these people coming in now could be Gerald Parker?"

◇

"Whose idea was it to come to Madame bloody Tussauds on a Sunday?" Bobbi whinged a bit later, after they'd dropped Jo's bag at the hotel.

"It's probably going to be like this any day," Jo replied, not really listening. There was a long queue despite their buying tickets online and collecting them for their designated time slot. Ahead of them in the line, a couple held hands. They kept smiling stupidly at each other.

"You're not interested in the Marvel movie thing, are you?" Bobbi was asking. "Because I think we could give that a miss. How about the Queen? We should get a photo with the Queen."

"Mmmm," Jo replied. She watched as the guy draped an arm over his girlfriend's shoulder and pulled her closer. She leant her head against his shoulder. It was hard to watch and Jo looked away. Without realising it previously, she knew that she'd started to think about possibilities for the future. Not even necessarily the long-term future but she'd definitely been feeling like she could fall in love with Kelly. Of course, not all men were cheats, she knew that. Maybe there was just something about her that attracted that type? Gullible and trusting, willing to throw herself at someone without asking enough questions first? Or had Kelly just thought she was out for a good time, no strings attached? It's not like they'd talked about it.

The line started to move. Then stop. Then move again. Finally they got through the door.

"It's kind of creepy," Bobbi said, after they'd taken a selfie in front of Audrey Hepburn. "I keep expecting someone to reach out and tap me on the shoulder. Oh, look, there's ET and Elliot."

Neither of them had much tolerance for crowds so when some time later they came upon the One Direction boys, they decided they'd get a photo with Harry and then maybe a quickie with Adele and get out of there. It was awkward though, as Jo was trying to fit both her and Bobbi into the shot as well as Harry, who was sitting, so it wasn't easy to get the right angle.

Jo felt someone tugging on her shirt.

"'Scuse me, miss, do you want me to take a photo for you?" The young boy gave her an angelic smile. He looked like a little cherub, Jo thought, with a mop of blond curls and large, blue eyes.

"Oh, would you? Thanks, sweetheart."

The boy took the phone from Jo, insisting he knew how to use it when she tried to explain how the camera worked. She stepped back, next to Bobbi. As they crouched down one on either side of Harry, he turned and swiftly fled into the crowd, taking her phone with him. Jo and Bobbi were left gaping stupidly after him.

"Oi, hey you. Come back, you little shitbag!" Jo yelled, causing a woman nearby with a small child to give her a furious glare.

Someone ahead cursed as the boy pushed past them. Jo could see him ducking and swerving through the crowd like a sewer rat. They took pursuit but soon had to give up. There were just too many people and he was small enough to slip amongst them. Plus, Bobbi couldn't run very fast in her heels.

"Damn, bugger, bloody fuck it," Jo swore. It felt like the last straw and she wanted to cry in frustration.

Bobbi put a soothing hand on Jo's shoulder and gave it a

sympathetic squeeze. "Shall we find security and report it? Or go to the police?"

"No," Jo sighed, "there's not much point. I reckon there's next to no chance of getting it back."

Bobbi agreed. "He's probably part of one of those child crime rings. He'll take it back to the lair and Fagin will give him a scrap of bread and a mug of tea."

Jo looked gloomy. "He's like the Jammie Dodger."

Bobbi guffawed. "You mean the Artful Dodger. I don't think a biscuit stole your phone."

"He looked so innocent. Just shows you shouldn't judge a book by its cover. It'll probably be reset to factory settings and sold by this afternoon."

Bobbi considered. "Yours probably wasn't the first phone he's stolen today. Probably uses his innocent looks to scam hundreds of people every week."

"In an awful way, that makes me feel slightly better. At least I'm not the only gullible one."

They came out into the street, but of course there was no sign of their little Artful Dodger anywhere.

"Speaking of Jammie Dodgers though," Bobbi was saying, "shall we go and get a coffee and something to eat? Or we've still got time to check out the Camden Markets if you're up to it?"

"Let's go to the markets. I might be able to find a cheap phone to buy."

"You might even be able to buy your own phone back."

◇

The bustle of the market was welcome in a way that the crowds at Madame Tussauds hadn't been. It was right up their alley.

Jo linked her arm through Bobbi's.

"It's so different to when I was here last. I bought a denim jacket with big brass buttons, which I thought was so edgy. Bayley found it hanging in the back of my wardrobe a couple of years ago. I think she still wears it."

She was feeling a bit chirpier. They'd eaten falafel at Basta and Jo had found a lovely silk scarf that wouldn't take up too much room in her suitcase. She was admiring the two new rings she had bought, holding her hand up so that they glittered in the sunlight. "I wonder if we might see any celebrities. I swear I saw Bob Geldof walking down the street one time."

"Perhaps Harry comes here on a Sunday to buy his tomatoes," Bobbi added, and they laughed so much about what they would say to him if he walked past right now that Jo spilt her takeaway coffee down the front of Bobbi's canary-yellow top.

CHAPTER 38

Bobbi

The next day, after a nice buffet breakfast, they went on a day tour Bobbi had booked them.

At the Tower of London they started at the iconic White Tower, the most famous castle keep in the world. Built to impress and intimidate, and full of king's armour.

Then on to the Tower Green where all the important executions had occurred, watched only by the privileged few, away from the crowds of peasants. Anne Boleyn and Catherine Howard had both been beheaded here, on order of their husband Henry VIII, and also Lady Jane Grey who was only sixteen at the time.

"I wish they had a fake hanging block here," lamented Bobbi. "That would make for a cool picture."

"Let's go look at the Traitors' Gate. It says in the brochure a 'water entrance to the Tower of London used to bring prisoners in. Once upon a time, the recently executed heads could be seen, held up on spikes.' Jesus. That would have been something to see."

"Ooh yes, very *Game of Thrones*."

They added on the Beefeaters audio tour, which was great, even if Bobbi had spent ten minutes trying to switch her headset from German into English. Still, she'd managed to ascertain that there were a few theories on why they were called beefeaters.

"I reckon the theory about them being paid in slabs of beef, to keep them strong, while the poor outside the gates lived on scraps, sounds the most likely," Bobbi declared as they wandered through the gift shop. "Too bad if you were a vegetarian."

"I doubt anyone was willingly a vegetarian then, Bob," Jo said scathingly. "Nah, I like the idea that King Henry was so paranoid about poisoning, he made them try his dishes first as a precaution. What a job — great, until it wasn't".

She and Jo purchased tacky, matching pyjamas that made them look like they were in the navy and red beefeater uniform. Well, they did if you squinted — or drank a lot first.

◇

They'd upgraded their tickets to get faster entry to Hampton Court and Kensington Palace and were glad of it. They were teeming with tourists. The crowds were insane, and neither Bobbi nor Jo had much patience for all the cameras and selfie sticks. Hampton Court was stunning, especially the gardens and maze, and its history was fascinating with its uses ranging from Shakespeare's theatre, and a banquet hall, to a prison. Jo loved the idea that Jane Seymour's ghost was still seen every year on the anniversary of her death. By the time they'd trooped around Kensington Palace, however, their enthusiasm was waning. It was a long day. They were getting hangry. And thirsty. Plus Bobbi needed a wee.

It was early evening and Bobbi's feet were killing her, so they stopped at Beer+Burger for some deep-fried jalapeños and a couple of beers. Jo ordered while Bobbi visited the ladies and then they sat and talked about their plans for the next day.

"You know what?" Jo said unexpectedly, banging her hand on the table, and sloshing her beer.

"I feel like getting shit-faced."

"Cocktails it is!" Bobbi said with enthusiasm.

◇

They were standing outside the hotel in the cold at four-thirty in the morning, wearing their matching beefeater pyjamas and hotel slippers. Jo's fringe was sticking straight up on one side. She had a toothpaste smear across her chin. Bobbi could see in the glass doors that her mascara was now at the highly unattractive panda stage. Her own braless state meant she had to keep her arms folded for support and hands strategically placed to cover cold nipples.

She was feeling either very tired, half asleep or still drunk. It was hard to tell. Jo kept swaying into her and hiccupping every few minutes.

There was the flash of a camera.

A tall woman in a beige suit, writing in a notebook, told them she was a reporter from the *Daily Dish*, and asked for their names. After several slurred attempts, Jo managed to spell them out.

"Nice pyjamas," she snorted. "Any idea what's happened here?" she turned to Bobbi to ask.

"Buggered if I know, we're just here to see Harry Styles."

The fire alarm cut off suddenly, leaving the night eerily quiet, aside from the murmur of traffic. Bobbi needed a Panadol and a large glass of water. They'd had *lots* of cocktails. There'd been dancing. Not much food, plus shots with a group of ladies having their 'book club'. They'd stopped for hot chips on the way home, and for Bobbi to pee down an alley, then fallen into bed, only to be jarred awake by the fire alarm what felt like minutes later.

The fire crew were still in the foyer, talking with the night manager. They had gone in to inspect the hotel and Bobbi was hoping they would say it was a false alarm so she could go back to sleep. With any luck, it would be back to her dream about Andre and the tub of chocolate ice cream.

The manager came out finally and the fire crew started to climb back into their truck. Apparently, she told them, apologising profusely, it was a rat that had chewed into the wiring.

"Gross," Jo slurred as they went back in to wait for the lift. "I hate rats, they're disgusting animals." Then she leant over and promptly threw up in the rubbish bin.

◇

The next morning they slept in. Jo was still drooling on her pillow when Bobbi finally had to get up for water and a wee. She was getting too old for all the drinking, she decided. When she got home she was going to do a detox.

She flicked on the jug, and while it boiled, had a bit of a sort out of her things, putting some clothes into a pile for washing, and chucking out receipts and things from her shopping. In one of the bags from the market was a pamphlet someone had handed her. It was for an open night at a local club for up-and-coming comedians. That could be a good plan for tonight. It seemed like Jo needed a laugh, since she was still down about Kelly.

She made tea, and put one next to Jo's bed, along with a water and a sleeve of Panadol in case she was as hungover as Bobbi. Sitting down on the bed to drink her own tea, she googled Harry again. She was hoping to find a picture of him with Andre and this time she hit pay dirt. There he was, following Harry down a street. Harry was carrying an iced coffee, looking cute and a little dishevelled, while Andre was looking very imposing and sexy. Bobbi saved the picture, then cropped it so it was just Andre, and set it as her screen saver. She felt about twelve, but she loved the feeling she got looking at him.

She'd have to remember to shave everything tomorrow.

CHAPTER 39

Jo

Bobbi trotted after Jo down Oxford Street. Jo was on a mission.

"Are you sure about this?" she asked Jo for the third time.

"Absolutely."

Earlier that day she had sat with her iPad balanced on her knee, cup of tea in hand, while she FaceTimed Bayley. It had been a good chat.

"Bay, I'm so sorry about the mix-up and what happened on *Seven Sharp*," she said straight off. Bayley laughed.

"That's okay, it was a bit of a shock to find out I'd died but that's all been sorted. Where am I, anyway? I hope you're treating me well and buying me lots of cocktails. Maybe a lovely new dress to cover up the bikini," she added hopefully.

Jo pulled a mock sad face. "Sorry to say Bay but you are officially dead now. You got thrown off a train outside of

Manchester and managed to grind British Rail to a halt in the process. I guess you'll have to make do with Sam, and Harry will have to find his own person."

"Speaking of Sam," Bayley replied a little awkwardly, "what do you think about all that?"

"I think it's great. I've always liked Sam and I just want you to be happy. Which I can tell you are."

Bayley grinned back at her. "I am. I've always liked him but I didn't really know how great he really was until we started to work together. We have the same goals and we've got heaps in common. And it's been pretty cool not having Bobbi here being all suspicious and secret squirrelly."

Jo laughed. "At least it will stop her going on about her famous gaydar for a bit. That one threw her for six."

They both giggled at the thought of Bobbi being dumbfounded about being wrong. For a change. From across the room Bobbi looked up from the book she'd been reading and shot her daggers. Jo smiled sweetly at her and then said to Bayley, "Bobbi sends her love, by the way."

"So Scotland looked cool. And now you've got, what, one more concert?"

"Yep, one more concert."

Bayley got up and carried her laptop with her into the kitchen, past Sam who was sitting at the table surrounded by papers. Accounts, Jo guessed. He gave her a little wave as Bayley passed by. Bayley placed her laptop on the counter and Jo watched as she flicked on the jug and took two mugs down from the shelf, opened a canister on the counter and extracted two tea bags which she placed in the cups. Watching Bayley do these banal, everyday things made her feel kind of homesick, just for a fleeting few seconds. She wished she could be there with her having a cup of tea, but the feeling was gone as quickly as it had come.

Jo told her about losing her phone and about finding Mona in her suitcase.

"I can't decide whether travelling with you and Aunty Bob would be amusing or just an embarrassing disaster waiting to happen," Bayley said, rolling her eyes. "Why do these things never happen to other people? Normal people."

"We're perfectly normal," Jo protested.

"You two should be forced to wear a warning."

Bayley picked up both mugs of tea and gave one to Sam, resting her hand briefly on his shoulder before she took her own tea back into the living room.

"Bay," Jo said, once Bayley had plonked herself into one of Bobbi's overstuffed blue chintz armchairs. "Something kind of ... happened in Scotland — between me and Adam's dad, Kelly. You probably don't really want to know but—"

Bayley's eyes widened in surprise. "Eurgh, Mum — just don't go into detail, okay?"

"You're not shocked?"

"Surprised, I guess. But it's cool. You deserve to be happy too after Dad screwed you over like he did."

Jo sighed and looked down at her cup. "Yeah. It didn't

work out but I think I would have quite liked it to be something more."

Jo didn't want Bayley to see how upset she was, not wanting to put a dampener on her newfound happiness. Bayley probably wouldn't have noticed though, even if she hadn't plastered a smile on her face. But Jo was genuinely pleased to see her looking so blissful.

"I guess you should look at it positively. The start of your new life. Embrace it for what it was," Bayley was saying. Then she paused and said, sincerely, "I think you're quite brave actually, Mum. Good for you."

"Brave? Me?"

"Yeah, it takes guts to put yourself out there. Especially at your age."

"Well, thanks, Bay. That's great," Jo laughed.

Jo had thought about what Bayley had said after they'd disconnected and decided she was right. Whatever it had been that she'd had with Kelly, she had to look at it as a positive experience. It made her realise she had started a new chapter of her life. She could change things in her life that she wasn't happy about. Being in your forties didn't mean your life was over. In fact, your life was never over, until it was.

◇

So now, here they were, hurrying down Oxford Street to an appointment at the tattoo parlour.

"This is crazy, you've never liked tattoos," Bobbi was saying. She'd decided to get one too, so Jo had booked for both of them.

"I've kind of grown used to them lately," Jo replied with a smirk.

Bobbi quickly decided on a sunflower on her shoulder and was taken into a cubicle, leaving Jo to flick through a book of designs. She was pretty sure she knew what she wanted and she finally found it.

Jo's tattoo artist was Chance, a beefy guy covered with some impressive ink and quite a few intimidating-looking piercings himself. He told her he could do it on the spot, as she'd chosen a pretty standard design.

"Virgin then?" he asked her with a grin.

"W-what?" Jo sputtered.

"First tattoo, yeah?"

"Oh. Yes." She felt surprisingly calm, not freaking out and overthinking like she normally would. She was doing something that she wanted. Something that would be an indelible reminder of this trip, always.

"I'll be gentle with you." Chance gave her a huge grin.

He spent some time preparing the design and printing it out and then very carefully placed it onto Jo's skin. He showed it to her in a mirror to make sure she was happy with the placement, which she was. He got started and Jo realised she'd braced herself for a painful experience but it wasn't at all. There was just a kind of a pricking sensation mainly and Chance kept her occupied chatting about his wife, who was a university lecturer, and their two young children. It turned out he was a sweet guy and very interesting too. He showed her his first tattoo, which a tattoo artist mate had given him, a complicated-looking dragon snaking down his ribs. Before Jo knew it he had wiped off the excessive ink and pulled out the mirror to show her his finished work.

"Wow. I really love it." She twisted for a better look. "It's perfect."

"I'll just get you some info on after-care and you're good to go."

Bobbi had finished just before Jo and was sitting waiting. She looked up questioningly and Jo grinned at her.

"I really thought you wouldn't go through with it," she told Jo as they paid.

Bobbi pulled down the sleeve of her top to show Jo her new design. "What do you think?"

"It's great."

Bobbi replaced her sleeve and they put their coats on. "Well?" Bobbi was looking at her expectantly.

"I can't show you here," Jo muttered. "It's on my bum."

Bobbi cackled. "We're going straight to get a coffee then and you can show me in the bathroom."

"That might be unhygienic," Jo protested, but Bobbi ushered her out the door, down the road and into the first decent cafe they came across where she hurriedly ordered them two coffees before manhandling Jo into the restrooms.

Jo unzipped her trousers and gingerly pulled them down.

Bobbi bent closer to look and then after a bit let out a whoop of laughter so loud it echoed around the small room. She covered her mouth with her hand.

"It's a moth!" she exclaimed, her eyes dancing with mischief.

"It is most certainly *not* a moth, it's a butterfly!" Jo retorted crossly.

"Sorry, Jo, but I think it's a moth."

Jo craned around to get a look at her arse in the mirror. No, it was definitely a butterfly.

"It looks a bit like Harry's," Bobbi decided. "Smaller of course. And I'll bet he has a nicer-looking bum."

Jo whacked her on the arm. "Thanks a lot." She strained for another look and decided she was very happy with the result, as far as she could see.

CHAPTER 40

Bobbi

They went to a restaurant called Bob Bob Ricard for a late lunch. The name seemed to be a sign. The decor was amazing, and they had a lobster mac 'n' cheese that was to die for. But the best part was the little button at their booth. If you pushed it, your lovely server would bring you a bottle of champagne. Genius. They each took a turn to do it. When in Rome, after all.

"Do you think I'm masculine, Jo?" Bobbi asked her halfway through the second bottle.

"What? No," Jo said looking surprised, "far from it."

"I mean, I just wonder if hanging round all the drag queens has changed my style. Maybe I'm too old now to dress the way I do? Mutton and lamb and all that."

Jo frowned. "Since when do you care what people think of you, Bobbi? Don't go changing. I love how much you express yourself. I think if anything it's me who needs to start caring less and expressing myself more."

"Yes but no one's ever mistaken you for a drag queen, have they?" Bobbi grumbled.

"Maybe not," Jo admitted, "but I often think I should have some of your girls give me styling tips. Perhaps Kiki — she's just gorgeous. It's not really an insult to be a queen, is it?"

They sipped their champagne and reflected for a moment.

"You're right," Bobbi announced. "Fuck it. Who's even judging me anyway?"

"Apart from Mum," Jo said drily.

"Another good reason not to conform," Bobbi agreed.

◇

They decided to walk back to the hotel, and as they ambled along the streets of Soho they passed a retro vintage boutique. The mannequin in the window was wearing a glamorous black dress and pearls.

"Oh, look, how gorgeous. Very Audrey Hepburn," said Jo. "Did you know she had really big feet?"

"Let's go in and try something on," Bobbi insisted. "It's the perfect opportunity for reinvention."

They wandered in and the sales assistant gave them a sunny smile.

"Hello, ladies," she said cheerfully "Are you happy to just browse?"

"We are, thanks," Bobbi replied as she flicked through a

rack of coats.

"Okay, just let me know if I can help. I'm Jane," she told them with a smile and went back to steaming a dress she had on a hanger.

Jo pulled out another black dress and asked Bobbi what she thought.

"It's nice," Bobbi told her, "but you always wear black."

Jo kept looking and pulled out one in a burnt orange. "Oh, look at this one. I love it," she enthused, "but where would I wear it?"

"Just try it on anyway," Bobbi encouraged her.

It looked gorgeous. Even Jo had to admit it did great things for her.

"Actually," she called out to Jane, "could I try the pearls on with this? And maybe the shoes too, depending on the size?"

Jane took the necklace off the mannequin and checked the shoes. They were too small, but she had another pair she thought might work, and she gave them to Jo to try on.

"Pearls are making such a comeback right now," she told them.

Bobbi laughed. "She just wants them 'cause Harry Styles wears them," she told Jane.

"Oh, I adore him," Jane enthused. "His dress sense is amazing. I wish I knew where he got the jumper with the baby chicken on it."

"Gucci would be my guess."

Jo ended up buying the lot. Dress, pearls and shoes, as well as a pair of tartan trousers she spotted. Bobbi got a funky pillbox handbag and a gorgeous red velvet coat with a pink lining. She'd have to wear it home, she thought, as they continued on their way.

Jo had gone a bit quiet and Bobbi wondered if she was thinking about Kelly again.

"How do you feel about stand-up comedy?" she asked Jo as they walked.

"Oh, maybe."

"It'll be fun," Bobbi said cheerfully.

"I suppose so," Jo said. "Why not? How bad can it be?"

◇

They really hadn't planned on drinking much more that night, but the stand-up 'comedy' was pretty dire.

So far, they'd had one guy whose whole set had been 'yo momma' jokes, a dreadlocked chick with a monologue about periods, and now a very, very drunk lad with friends who were heckling and carrying on so much, they hadn't actually caught a punch line yet.

They resorted to doing a shot between gins in a vain attempt to make it seem funnier.

There were still three acts to go. They had to hope the performances were in order from bad to good, not bad to worse, but didn't hold out much hope.

The MC for the night, Bryce, looked like a caricature of a used car salesman: Brylcreemed hair and nylon suit, with a bad-taste 'sexy woman' tie and shiny faux crocodile shoes.

He came back on with some lame banter and then announced the next act. "This is a bloke all the way from down the road, let's give it up for my mate, Gerald Parker!"

Jo spat her gin across the table in a wide arc of spray that even Harry would have been impressed with.

Surely not, thought Bobbi. There must be a few Gerald Parkers after all.

A balding, podgy guy in a pair of mustard-coloured trousers and a too-tight, cream turtleneck came mincing onto the stage. He had large ears and small eyes, and when he smiled, all his teeth looked like tiny, baby ones.

"Thank you, thank you," he said in a squeaky voice like a chipmunk. "A funny thing happened to me on the train—"

Bobbi and Jo started to laugh. Bobbi was laughing so hard she had to cross her legs tightly to ensure she didn't pee herself. Jo was shaking and crying and they couldn't stop. The peals of laughter got louder and louder, until they were roaring. Bobbi had knocked her glass over and the liquid was trickling onto the already sticky carpet. Sometimes this happened to them. The more they tried to contain themselves, the worse it got. Every time they looked at each other it would set them off again. Eventually, their waiter came over and politely asked them to leave.

This seemed even funnier as they stood outside the theatre, leaning against the wall snorting and wheezing. Eventually Jo managed to get out, "Fancy being kicked out of a comedy club for laughing too much."

This set them off with another round until Bobbi's stomach was aching. A couple walked past and the man said to his date, "See, I told you we should have gone in, it's obviously brilliant." Bobbi couldn't help it. She laughed so much that she'd had to beg them to let her back in for a wee.

CHAPTER 41

Adam

Adam did his first set at the pub on Saturday night. He stuck to older songs to suit the crowd, and they seemed to enjoy it. Mary and Joan had even got up for a bit of a boogie and dragged their husbands with them. Colleen had given him a Coke and a plate of chips halfway through while he took a break and told him that if the feedback was good, he could sing there on weekends when he was home.

◇

He caught up on most of his school work except maths. He was pretty sure he was going to fail that anyway though, and doubted it would be a requirement for any of the music courses he was looking at, so he was just ignoring that.

Things were going well. He and his da were getting on better. He was in a good place.

But, his da was moping. He was pretending he was fine, but he wasn't. He'd gone mostly quiet but also flew off the handle over minor stuff. Like toothpaste in the sink and wet towels on his bed. Later, he'd be overly nice, saying sorry and letting Adam have a beer with dinner and not nagging him to go to bed. Adam could see he was miserable and decided that he'd have to take action. He'd tried texting Jo but hadn't heard back from her. He'd never gotten Bobbi's number.

He made dinner. Spag bol again. It was really the only thing he could make except pancakes and toasted sandwiches.

While they were eating he asked, "Heard from Jo?" and Kelly looked up sharply.

"Nae, why? Have you?"

"Da," he started, "did you stuff it up?"

Kelly looked startled, then tried to compose his face before saying "I dinnae ken what your gettin' at lad."

Adam sighed. "I know you two were, you know, like, lovers or whatever," he said awkwardly. "I saw Jo in the hallway one night — anyway, I know. And she's nice. I overheard her at the station and—" He trailed off, not really sure what to say.

Kelly rubbed at his face miserably. "For some reason Bobbi thinks I'm with Finella and Jo thinks I'm scum for cheating."

"Finella? Who the hell's Finella?"

"She's an old friend from school who I went on a couple of dates with. She got a bit clingy and I don't think I handled it well."

"Well, why would she think you were dating her now?"

"I dinnae know, lad, but they had lunch where she worked, then she turned up here when they were leaving."

"It's probably just shite village gossip, Da."

"Aye, I've tried ringing, even left her three messages, but she's not answering. I dinnae ken where she's staying."

"Do you like her though?" Adam pressed.

"Aye, I like her a lot."

"Right then." Adam stood to clear the plates. "We need a plan."

Kelly looked a bit lost. "What do you mean?"

"To get her back," Adam called over his shoulder. "We're going to hafta do something big. Something romantic. So she knows you're serious."

Kelly was sitting at the table still when he came back.

"So, what were you thinking?" he asked quietly, perhaps hopefully.

This was going to be perfect, thought Adam. His dad would have to let him go to the concert tomorrow night now. And he'd need to find his fabric pens.

"Well," Adam said, "I have two tickets to Harry Styles' London show and we know who else is going, so ..."

He couldn't wait to tell Thomas. He could meet him in London for sure now. They had texted quite a few times, and talked about coming out, and how the guys were at school. He was going to be brave like Thomas and just do it. He was feeling pretty confident about things now. He figured he could handle anyone being a dick. People were dicky about lots of shite at school, even about girls, so he wasn't too fazed. He was kind of missing the band too and looking forward to getting back and jamming with them. Thomas had said they were a bit shit without him.

◇

He rang Hannah and told her about his plan to go to music school.

"Mum would have loved that," she told him.

Then he told her he was gay. She was all 'whatever' — she was more interested in the gossip about Jo and Kelly. He told her about the extra 'Scottishness' their da had developed, which they both cracked up about, and how he'd caught Jo sneaking out of Kelly's room, which wasn't something either of them wanted to dwell on, they decided.

"So, what's she like?" Hannah asked.

"She's really nice, I think you'd like her. But she's gone off to London thinking Da has a girlfriend."

"Oh shite. Poor Da."

"Don't worry, I've got a plan. I'm taking Da to Harry's final concert so he can find her."

'What, so you're just gonna turn up and find her amongst the thousands of people there?"

"Well, if you've got a better idea ..."

"Can't you just go to the hotel with flowers? Wouldn't that be what a normal person would do?"

"Except we don't know where they're staying, Einstein.

I've got Jo's number but she's not answering and I don't have Bobbi's."

"Well, I guess it won't hurt to try the concert."

"Yeah, and bonus, I get to go and see Harry."

"Yeah, with your da," Hannah laughed.

CHAPTER 42

Jo

Jo woke with no tattoo regrets the next morning and kept going to the mirror to get a better look, which she suspected was irritating Bobbi.

"Can you just get dressed so we can go out?" she said. "I'm starving."

Jo took one last furtive but satisfied look and pulled on her jeans.

The concert was that night and they had no real plans for the day, so after breakfast they decided to walk around the Tate Modern art gallery and then have a nosy in Harrods. Mum had requested they buy her something from there, so they needed to find something that looked the part without breaking the bank. Whatever they bought would have to have the Harrods logo, she and Bobbi agreed, so that Mum could show it off to all her friends.

They'd gone to a Boots pharmacy and stocked up on Panadol — they seemed to have gone through an alarmingly large amount — and then to an Apple store where Jo bought a new phone.

Maybe she wasn't cut out for any kind of a short-term relationship, Jo thought. She just couldn't separate her feelings from the physical. In a year or so, when she was back home sitting at her desk proofreading a manual for *Small Business Management for Dummies*, or something equally scintillating, perhaps she'd remember her time in Scotland with fondness. Right now, it was just a bit too raw.

Then again, maybe in a year she wouldn't be sitting at home proofreading. She could sell the house, Jo thought. Maybe it was time to move away, get a fresh start.

She thought again about Kelly's distillery, and how much she would love to do something where she could use her general knowledge skills. Perhaps do something involving more interaction with people. She really was a people person, and working from home was very solitary.

Jo drifted into a fantasy where she was living in the countryside, running tours and making high teas. Funny though; in this daydream, all her settings seemed to be next to the sea, have lighthouses, or very Scottish-looking villages. There may even have been a flock of nesting shags — or guillemots — in one of them. Shaking herself from her reverie she tried to muster some enthusiasm for what Bobbi was saying.

"Jo!" Bobbi sighed. "If you're not going to even listen, I'm going to choose the restaurant for lunch. Where was your head anyway?"

"I don't care where we go for lunch; you choose if you like." Jo looked at Bobbi thoughtfully. "Do you think I could teach adult classes, or something like that?"

"What? What brought that on?"

"I don't know really, I'm thinking I might change a few things when I get home. Do something different."

"Yeah, 'course you could. You've always loved imparting your knowledge on people. You do it all the time, I can attest to that."

Jo swatted her.

"Seriously though, you'd be great at anything like that."

"Hmm. I guess there are heaps of options I'd never thought about before. When we took that tour in Manchester, I thought I could have done a much better job of it."

"I'm sure you would have. You'll have to work on the accent though."

Jo shot her a look.

"Come on then Bob, let's go and have some lunch. We might not get time to eat much later on. And you know what? I think I'm going to choose where we go after all." She linked her arm through Bobbi's, feeling slightly better. Bobbi knew she'd been feeling a bit down and Jo appreciated she'd been trying to cheer her up. Whatever happened, they'd always have each other and that meant the world to Jo.

◇

While they ate, they discussed what Harry might be wearing that night. She and Bobbi liked to have a guess each and then see who had got the closest. The winner was supposed to buy a round of drinks but so far they'd both been so far off the mark they couldn't have picked between them. Harry sure liked to surprise them.

"Shall we go and get our nails done after this?" Jo suggested.

"Oh yes, great idea," Bobbi agreed. "I might get a pedicure too."

"Harry might be in getting his done too," Jo said with a laugh as she got out her phone to google some pictures of Harry's nails. They oohed and ahhed over his hands for a bit.

"You know what I love about Harry?" Bobbi announced.

"I think the list might be smaller if we went with what we don't love," Jo said with a grin.

"Well, true," Bobbi said, "but I just really love when he's talking, in an interview or something, and he does that thing when he answers a question, and he says 'Well, I mean ...'"

"Oh, yes," Jo agreed. "It's just so him. Classic Harry Styles saying."

They kept eating.

"Actually, Bobbi," Jo noted, "you've started saying that quite a lot too. It's rubbed off."

"Has it?" Bobbi contemplated. "I mean ..."

They laughed.

"It's just so much cooler when it's Harry though," Jo declared.

"Isn't everything?"

They both sighed wistfully.

CHAPTER 43

Bobbi

They were due to fly home two days after Harry's final London concert with a stopover in Singapore for a couple of nights. Bobbi was wishing they could stay longer and contemplating suggesting to Jo that they extend things and do some more of Europe first. Sam had everything running smoothly at the bar, and there wasn't much else to get back for that couldn't wait.

◇

She was trying not to think too much about Andre. She didn't want to get her hopes up. He might not be there. He might not see her at all. She may have just imagined he was interested. But she shaved and moisturised and deep-conditioned her hair that morning anyway. Just in case. And she was planning on wearing her sexiest underwear too. Think positive, after all.

The afternoon had flown by. The Tate had been incredible.

The Andy Warhol exhibition was fantastic and the Zanele Muholi photography had been mind-blowing, stunningly beautiful pieces of art. They'd spent at least an hour just on those alone.

Harrods had felt a bit blah after that, so they'd gone in and found a wine carry bag with the fancy logo on it, shelled out their fifty pounds and left fairly quickly. It was all very exorbitant and self-indulgent, the whole 'posh' thing, they'd agreed. Cheap and cheerful was more their style.

"Where shall we eat?" Bobbi asked as they arrived back at the hotel with their shopping.

"Somewhere cheap and easy but with cocktails," Jo decided, "and maybe potato skins?"

"Sounds perfect," Bobbi agreed.

The concierge called out to them as they passed the reception.

"Excuse me, is either of you Jo?"

"Yes, that's me."

He handed Jo a folded sheet of hotel stationery. "A young lady left you this earlier today."

"Who's leaving you notes in London?" Bobbi asked, puzzled.

"I won't know until I read the bloody thing, will I?" Jo replied crossly.

"Well, don't open it until we're sitting down in case it's bad news."

◇

Bobbi threw her handbag onto the table and flopped down on the bed while Jo opened the envelope and started to read. "It's from Hannah, Kelly's daughter."

"Come on, read it out loud," Bobbi replied impatiently.

"Hi, Jo, you don't know me but this is Hannah, Kelly's daughter. He's here in London hoping to find you. There seems to have been a big misunderstanding but I promise you he doesn't have a girlfriend. If you want to get in touch, he and Adam are staying at the Stadium Crown Hotel. I really hope you get this, and things work out for you guys. Regards, Hannah Kinnard."

"Wow." Bobbi looked over at Jo when she'd finished reading.

"Oh, my God, find me the number for the Stadium Crown. I've got to ring him now."

Jo dialled the number and waited while the receptionist put her through to Kelly's room, Bobbi hovering over her shoulder. It rang and rang but there was no reply.

"Try his mobile."

Jo picked up her phone before remembering she didn't have any numbers stored.

"Shit, his number is in my old phone."

"Look," said Bobbi, glancing at her watch, "we need to get going soon. How about we try after dinner and if we still can't reach him, we'll go to the hotel first thing in the morning."

"Why didn't I ask him about Finella at the station? He must think I'm an idiot."

"Well, clearly not if he's followed you all the way to London."

"I don't understand. Why would Joan have said he was with Finella?"

Bobbi thought for a bit. "She definitely said they dated in high school and got back together after his wife died. I guess that doesn't mean they're still seeing each other now though."

"I suppose when you think about it, it's a bit strange that she was never around."

"Or on our quiz team."

"He did say something when we went for dinner about not having a serious relationship since Linda died. God, why do I always jump to conclusions? I should have trusted him more."

"Nobody could blame you after Marcus. Don't beat yourself up about it now. Anyway, let's just go and enjoy this last concert, knowing that you can sort it all out tomorrow."

"You're right. And on a positive note, we don't have to lug Bayley around with us any more."

"Poor Harry. He doesn't know what he's missed out on. Actually, I feel kind of bad. It might be my fault I got the wrong end of the stick from Joan." Bobbi looked sideways at Jo. "But if you'd told me you were shagging him, I might have questioned her more."

CHAPTER 44

Bayley

Bayley was in love. Food tasted even better than usual. Life was more positive. Even rain seemed more romantic than miserable. Sex was incredible. Having someone to run you a bath after work was heaven. She and Sam were getting on so well and had talked about getting a place together when Bobbi got back.

Damn, Bayley thought. I forgot to tell Bobbi about Hilary.

She'd sent a snarky email to *Seven Sharp* after the piece featuring her cardboard likeness screened, telling them they should fact-check better and that she was, in fact, alive and well.

To her surprise, she'd received a reply, and it was from Hilary Barry. She was lovely and apologetic and asked if Bayley wanted to be interviewed for a follow-up piece.

They'd done a small clip at the bar and it would be playing

tonight. She thought Aunty Bob would love that. Free publicity too, since a couple of the queens had made an appearance. Hilary had asked her about her relationship with Sam, and how she thought Harry Styles would take it now that she was no longer in the market for love.

She was a laugh, Hilary. She could see why Jo and Bobbi had a bit of a girl crush on her.

But as she told Hilary, she and Harry would never have worked, and she figured Harry would do just fine on his own.

CHAPTER 45

Adam

They arrived in London in the late afternoon and Hannah had arranged to meet them for an early dinner. She had a friend she was keen to catch up with from school, and planned to go out with her after.

Adam and Kelly were already seated when Hannah finally arrived, grinning widely as she hugged Kelly and then squeezed herself into the booth next to Adam. She was all bouncy and smug looking, Adam noted.

"Sorry I'm late, but I'm pretty sure you'll forgive me after I tell you what I've just done. I know I'm already your favourite child but you're not going to believe this. I think I've found Jo," she told Kelly, pulling out her phone as she sat. "Check this out."

They both bent over the screen.

A newspaper article showed a grainy photo of Jo and Bobbi, looking a little dishevelled, wearing matching pyjamas and staring glassy-eyed into the camera. The headline read 'Hotel Hazard Leaves Harry Fans Caught In Their Hosiery'.

"Jesus Christ," Adam exclaimed. "Is that them?"

"Aye, it's not the most flattering photo, but that's them." Kelly took the phone to read the article.

"I went to the hotel but they weren't there so I left a note. Hopefully she'll ring you."

"Well, that's if we don't see her at the concert first," Adam added.

"Thanks, kids, I appreciate the support." Kelly smiled at them both.

Hannah patted his arm. "We're just so pleased to see you moving on since mam. It's about time, Da."

Then they all got a bit stupid and teary and had to have a family hug in the middle of bloody Planet Hollywood, which was 'so gay', Adam declared, just to get a laugh out of them.

After dinner they said goodbye to Hannah before heading off to the concert.

◇

Thomas was meeting him there. He'd texted Adam saying he was hanging to see him, and Adam had texted back 'me too', as well as a little heart emoji after it. He hoped Thomas didn't think that was weird or too much.

Adam was excited and nervous about seeing him, and nervous and excited for his da.

He'd made Kelly a T-shirt. He used one of Kelly's pale-grey Henleys and a neon-pink fabric pen to write in large block letters 'JO, JUST LET ME ADORE YOU'.

Kelly had protested that it was a dumb thing to write, but then, he didn't know Harry's lyrics like Adam and Jo did. Jo would get it.

"I've never felt less cool," grumbled Kelly and looked baffled when Adam had laughed so hard his Coke threatened to reappear.

He had suggested his da take a big bunch of sunflowers with him, but it was the wrong time of year. They'd probably be awkward to carry too and would just have ended up getting crushed.

The stadium was packed as usual. The vibe was really electric tonight, being the last show for the UK leg of the tour. There was no sign of Jo and Bobbi. Adam hoped they didn't have seated tickets. That would make it way harder to find them. He hadn't actually thought of a contingency plan if they couldn't see them.

Adam had arranged to meet Thomas by one of the merchandise stands, and he was glad when his da told him to go, that he'd get a drink and wait for him at the entrance to their section.

He was wearing the T-shirt Jo had paid for, and his skinny jeans, with a jacket. He didn't know what to do with his hands as he leant against the wall, trying to look casual and relaxed. He hoped he wasn't sweating, and then worried about his breath.

When he saw Thomas though, he suddenly felt really calm. Thomas was smiling at Adam a little shyly and Adam's heart was pounding, but in a cool way.

Thomas stopped in front of him. He looked like he was going to hug him, then changed his mind. "Sorry," Thomas said a little awkwardly instead. "Hi," he continued, "fuck, sorry, I'm kinda nervous."

Thomas looked around them as if he was worried someone might see them. Then Adam realised he was probably worried on Adam's behalf rather than his own, since Adam wasn't 'out' and Thomas was.

Fuck it, Adam thought. YOLO and all that. He leant in and kissed Thomas. On the mouth. It was brilliant. Especially when Thomas got over the shock and kissed him back. It was a proper kiss too. He even put his hands one on each side of Adam's face. He tasted like strawberry bubblegum.

Adam was definitely, 100% gay.

◇

They headed over to meet Kelly eventually, Adam apologising for throwing Thomas in the deep end, with a 'meet my dad' right off the bat. Thomas didn't seem too worried though, especially when Adam had taken his hand to lead him to the doors. He held on even when he introduced them, and Kelly had been fine, not even embarrassing at all. He even got them both a beer, which was mint.

They were in the mosh, and the crowds were going crazy. Kelly told him not to worry too much about him, to just enjoy the show, and Thomas, and he'd just look for Jo. They arranged to meet outside if they got separated. He and Thomas danced and sang and looked at each other a lot and grinned, and it was so perfect.

◇

Harry was taking a break between songs and doing a bit of audience interaction. Adam loved when he did that. Asking them questions and having a bit of banter in his lazy drawl.

Right now, he was pointing at someone nearby when Adam heard him say:

"So, who's this Jo then?"

CHAPTER 46

Bobbi

Andre was there. At the concert. He was hotter even than she'd remembered. Bobbi was having a hard time concentrating on the show when all she was thinking about was how to get near him. She was sure she'd seen him looking at her at one point.

They were quite far back in the mosh, and he was up front, looking all he-man and oozing masculine pheromones.

She was daydreaming of the two of them, all sweaty and tousled and him with his big hands all over her, when Jo grabbed her arm. Hard.

"Did he just say my name?" she hissed.

"Who?" Bobbi hadn't been listening.

"Harry! I swear he just said my name."

"Geez, calm down. You're probably not the only Jo in the audience."

"Oh, my God, is that—?"

Bobbi looked up at where Jo was pointing to the big screen.

It was Kelly, looking faintly awkward among a mass of younger people. The camera was zooming in on him as he spoke to Harry.

And then Andre was on screen, moving the hordes, pulling Kelly along, and the crowds were parting, like a little, narrower Red Sea, towards them. And her heart was pounding with excitement.

Then they were there. She thought maybe Kelly was kissing Jo. Bobbi was just staring up at Andre and he was grinning. A proper, big, sexy grin. Then he reached out for her wrist, pulling her forward and he had a marker that he was using to write something on the inside of her arm.

Then he bent down and whispered in her ear. "Been lookin' for you, darlin'. Meet me here, will ya? After the show."

And he was gone, pushing back towards the stage, the crowd going nuts around her, as Harry cheered on Kelly and Jo, before starting up his next song. But Bobbi was just looking at her arm, the warmth of Andre's hand spinning through her, into other areas of her body, and she was grinning like a maniac. On her arm was an address. And under that, the words 'As you wish'.

CHAPTER 47

Jo

It was insane. Everything had happened so quickly. One minute she'd been singing along to 'To Be So Lonely' feeling a bit teary and emotional and then Harry had been talking to the audience, in that lovely intense way he had that must have made the person he was talking to feel like they were the only one in the room. She and Bobbi were some way back from the front and near the edge, but there was a large screen at the side of the stage, which Jo was looking at now.

"So, who's this Jo then?"

Jo vaguely recalled thinking how thrilling it must feel to be the person he was talking to, before realising that he'd just said her name.

Harry was leaning into the audience, an amused look on his face. The cameras panned into the crowd then honed in on a single person. Jo gasped. Kelly suddenly appeared on the screen, as large as a multi-storey building. Harry had been focusing on his T-shirt, which in large vivid pink lettering said 'JO, JUST LET ME ADORE YOU'. Kelly looked a bit bewildered at the attention.

She squeezed Bobbi's arm so hard that Bobbi gave a small yelp.

"Are they here tonight? They are? Right, let's find this Jo and Bonnie. Jo? Where are you, Jo?" Harry was saying.

Someone seemed to catch Harry's eye then and Andre came into view on the screen, looking like a living mountain. He lifted a finger. He and Harry exchanged glances, Andre indicating something or someone with a flick of his eyes.

"Make way, make way," Harry was saying, waving his arms like he was clearing a path or perhaps doing breaststroke and grinning wildly from the stage.

Then Andre was coming towards them. And Kelly was with him. They were almost in front of them now. Andre was possibly smiling, Jo wasn't paying much attention to him though, it was Kelly she was looking at. He was staring straight at her, smiling tentatively, his lovely hazel eyes boring into her. He took the last few steps towards her and pulled her into his arms, wrapping them around her and kissing her. The crowd cheered, loudly, but Jo and Kelly just carried on, oblivious.

"Hey. Enough of that, this is a family show!" Harry called out, but she was unaware of what he said after that because all she could hear was the blood thumping in her ears as the band started playing again. The camera panned over Mitch, the guitarist, whose expression probably hadn't changed throughout the whole interaction and then on to Harry who had launched into the next song but was looking rather pleased with himself.

Kelly pulled away from her slightly and grinned stupidly. "I can't believe I found you."

"I'm so sorry," Jo told him, "I'm an idiot."

"Nae, I'm sorry, I shouldn't have let you leave like that," he murmured into her ear.

And then he kissed her again.

Epilogue

The pub was busy for a Thursday night, everyone jostling and laughing and it was hard to even get a space at the bar.

Adam was back at school, and starry-eyed with first love.

Bobbi had the contented look of a woman well shagged. She and Andre had seen a fair bit of each other over the past couple of days and had made plans for him to visit her in Wellington that summer, where Bayley and Sam were most likely fast asleep in their own love nest.

Kelly had gone home that morning. Jo was looking forward to heading back to St Abbs the next day to see where the relationship went. She suspected she may not be going home for a while.

She and Bobbi were at the bar, waiting to order another round of cocktails.

A very cute young man reached across Jo to hand the barman a tip, apologising to them as he did.

He was the spitting image of Harry, Jo thought. She had been telling Bobbi just a couple of days ago about a guy who lived locally that was such a good likeness that people often confused him for the real Harry. She nudged Bobbi and whispered, "It's lookalike guy."

Bobbi looked him over and whispered back, "Wow, he's even gone as far as getting matching tattoos."

"I doubt they're real," Jo replied dubiously.

He turned and caught her eye. "You know," she told him, "you really do have quite a remarkable likeness. You're almost as good looking as the real Harry Styles."

He gave her a bemused look.

"I mean ..." he started with a slow drawl, giving them a beaming smile.

About the authors

Nikki and Kirsty are sisters from New Zealand who decided to write a book about Harry Styles in the hope that he will play himself in the subsequent movie.

This is how it turned out.

You can find out more about us at
www.nikkiperryandkirstyroby.com

Milton Keynes UK
Ingram Content Group UK Ltd.
UKHW042033071123
432164UK00004B/244

9 780473 594626